★ "A wonderful story of triumph over imperfection, shame, and loss. . . . The author writes with empathy, honoring the possibilities of even peripheral characters; Kevin and Max are memorable and luminous. Many... novels deal with the effects of a friend dying, but this one is somewhat different and very special."
— *School Library Journal,* starred review

■ "Told by Max in retrospect, the story is both riveting and poignant, with solid characters, brisk pacing, and even a little humor to carry us along."
— *Booklist,* boxed review

◆ ". . . mesmerizingly suspenseful . . . Easily read but compelling: an intriguing and unusual story."
— *Kirkus Reviews,* pointed review

"The book is . . . compelling, with the outrageous grotesquerie of the partnership conveyed enjoyably in Max's narration. . . . Sort of *A Separate Peace* meets *Of Mice and Men . . .*"
— *BCCB*

"*Freak the Mighty* by Rodman Philbrick . . . is a winner. From the opening paragraphs, this book has a distinctive 'voice' as Philbrick develops his unusual characters. . . . In the hands of a lesser writer, these characters might have become clichés, but Philbrick develops an engaging story as this unlikey pair form a friendship and eventually combine forces to become Freak the Mighty."

— *Santa Cruz County Sentinel*

"Told from Max's perspective, the harrowing events of his life are revealed gradually, as he is able to face them, thanks to the wisdom of his friend who had taught him to 'think your way out of the pain.' A fascinating excursion into the lives of people whose freakishness proves to be a thin cover for their very human condition."

— *The Horn Book Magazine*

"The unique voice of this first-person narrative is fresh, funny, and touching. . . . The well-paced, compelling story leaves the reader feeling privileged to have shared the friendship of Freak the Mighty. *Highly Recommended.*"

— *Book Report*

"This is a touching story of strength, vulnerability, and friendship."

— *Language Arts*

Max
the
Mighty

POINT SIGNATURE EDITIONS

The Road Home
by Ellen Emerson White

From the Notebooks of Melanin Sun
by Jacqueline Woodson

Probably Still Nick Swansen
by Virginia Euwer Wolff

Dove and Sword
by Nancy Garden

The Wild Hunt
by Jane Yolen

I Can Hear the Mourning Dove
by James Bennett

Max
the
Mighty

Rodman Philbrick

Scholastic Inc.

New York Toronto London Auckland Sydney
Mexico City New Delhi Hong Kong Buenos Aires

Thanks to Kathryn Lasky,
who pointed me in the right direction.

This book was originally published in hardcover by The Blue Sky Press in 1998.

ISBN-13: 978-0-590-57964-3
ISBN-10: 0-590-57964-9

30 29 28 27 26   18 19/0

Printed in the U.S.A.   23

Original Blue Sky Press edition designed by Elizabeth B. Parisi

1.
The Whole Weird World

My name is Maxwell Kane and the thing you should know about me is this: even though I'm a big dude with a face like the moon and ears that stick out like radar scoops and humongous feet like the abdominal snowman, inside I'm a real weenie. A yellow-bellied sapsucker. A gigantic wuss. A coward.

I'll do just about anything to avoid a fight. I'm scared if I hit somebody, they might stay hurt forever, or worse. And then they'd haul me off to prison and everybody would say what did you expect, the boy is a bad apple just like his jailbird father.

Okay, maybe I am a little weird, but if you really think about it *everybody* is weird. That's the truth, and if you don't believe it then maybe you better listen up while I tell you about me and the

Bookworm and what happened when the whole weird world was out to get us.

It started like this. One day after school gets out I'm kind of moping along, minding my own business. Taking the long way home because there's nothing to do when I get there, so why hurry? I'm making sure not to step on any cracks and my brain is telling me don't be such a moron, it doesn't matter about cracks in the sidewalk. But my feet won't listen and they keep being careful, because you never know about cracks, do you?

Get a life, my brain says.

That's when I hear the girl screaming. She's not saying anything, just screaming so loud it puts a shiver in my bones. It makes me freeze up and not move and wish I could be invisible, or at least small. It makes me wish I could turn my ears off like you switch off a radio, and not hear anything. Most of all I want to run away and hide somewhere safe.

Because you can tell from the scream that somebody wants to hurt her.

2.

A Girl Called Worm

The girl keeps screaming and my brain is going, *Mind your own business. Somebody else can help her, not you.*

But there isn't anybody else and the screaming doesn't stop and before I know it my stupid feet start running over the cracks in the sidewalk, taking me closer and closer to trouble.

When I get to the corner of the block, I see this gang-banger messing around in the middle of the street. He's strutting around with his hands behind his back and he's got this sneering expression like he knows a really funny joke and you'll never get it.

"Keep screaming," he says. "Nobody cares."

The scream is coming from this skinny red-haired girl who's maybe eleven or twelve years old. She's got bright green eyes and freckles and her clothes are about two sizes too big and she's screaming bloody murder even though nobody's touching her.

"You big creep!" shouts the red-haired girl. "Lunk head! Bug brain! Give it back!"

"Louder," the gang-banger says. "I can't hear you."

Then he catches sight of me, and his grin gets wider and wider. "What do you know," he says. "Dinosaur boy to the rescue. I thought I felt the ground shaking."

Before I can stop my mouth from saying something stupid it goes, "Huh?"

The gang-banger loves it. "Huh?" he says. "Is that dinosaur talk for 'I'm retarded'?"

That's when I notice the skinny red-haired girl is staring at me. It's not a friendly kind of stare — she probably thinks I'm one of the gang-bangers, or maybe a retard like he says.

I go, "Leave her alone."

"Take it easy, Maxi Pad. We're just having a little fun," the gang-banger says. "You got a problem with that?"

The girl shakes her fist at him and goes, "Give it back or else."

The gang-banger looks at her puny little fist and smirks. "Oooh," he goes. "You gonna hit me?" Then he dances around, taunting her, and I see he's got hold of this small green backpack. A girl's backpack, for carrying school stuff.

4

"Give it back to her," I say.

He crosses his eyes and makes an oink-oink noise. "Pig boy," he says. "You better go home to Granny."

I try to grab it but he darts away, his teeth flashing white because he's having such a good time. "Moron Max," he laughs. "You're scaring me."

The red-haired girl makes a move but she can't touch him.

"Bookworm, bookworm, ugly little bookworm," he chants.

"Shut up!" she says. She's so mad her eyes look like they're full of green electricity.

"Worm girl!" the gang-banger cackles. "Whattaya have in here, worm food? Is that it?"

He opens up her backpack and roots around inside with this totally mean look on his face. Then he goes, "Whoa! What have we here?"

He pulls out a couple of paperback books and tosses them over his shoulder. Pages scatter and blow away like white leaves.

"Oh, you're real tough," the girl says. "You can beat up a book. I bet you never even *read* a book."

Then the gang-banger whistles and pulls something else out of the backpack. A hard plastic helmet with a light on the front, like miners wear so they can see in the dark.

"Don't you dare touch that!" the girl shouts. Then she goes mental and tries to grab the miner's helmet.

He grins and ducks away. "Finders keepers!" he shouts. "Losers weepers!"

But Worm isn't weeping, she's going nuts. Jumping up and trying to grab the helmet. He keeps dancing away, laughing in her face.

I wait my chance, and when he isn't looking I get behind him and lift the helmet off his head.

"Hey!" he bellows.

But I hold the miner's helmet up high and he can't reach it.

"Gimme that," he says, "or I'll punch your lights out."

"Try it."

The gang-banger curls up his fists and sets up on his feet like a boxer and for a moment I think he really is going to punch me. Then he looks at the girl and he looks at me and he spits on the ground by my feet.

"Who cares about your stupid junk," he says, and saunters away like he couldn't care less. Like he's the coolest dude in the whole wide world because he ripped up a book and scared an eleven-year-old girl.

The girl has eyes like green laser beams and this fierce look on her freckled face, like she thinks I'm the enemy, too.

I go, "Here," and give her the helmet.

The way she holds it in her hands, you know it means something special.

"What's it for?" I ask.

"None of your business," she says. And then she hugs the scratched-up old helmet to her chest and runs away, her thick red hair flying up like it wants to wave good-bye.

My brain didn't know it yet, but that's when trouble really started, the day I met a girl called Worm.

3.

Back to the Dark Down Under

The first thing I do when I get back to the down under is backflop on my bed and stare up at the ceiling while my brain goes, *You idiot, now the gang-bangers will be after you. You're toast, you mo-ron, toast!*

The down under is this room in the basement, with cheesy paneling and an old rug that smells like low tide. Not that I'm complaining. The down under is my very own place, my hidey-hole from the big bad world. My grandmother wants me to move upstairs, into the light of day, she says, but I tried that for a while and thanks but no thanks. If things get really bad I can still crawl under the bed and just veg out until my brain starts working again.

There's all kinds of books and games and junk lying around, but I'm not really in the mood. All I want to do is stare up at the ceiling and try to figure out why a scrawny girl would make such a big deal out of an old miner's helmet. I mean, she really went ballistic over it, right? Totally bonkers.

"Maxwell! Are you there?"

That's Gram, who raised me ever since my mom died. She's calling down from the cellar stairs like she always does. Just checking to see I'm not doing something stupid, like making my own firecrackers, which I don't do anymore since we had that small explosion. Really small, but I guess it sounded pretty bad from upstairs.

"Supper's almost ready!" she calls out in her cheery grandma voice. "Your favorite, spaghetti and meatballs!"

That hasn't been my favorite for about five years, but I haven't got the heart to tell Gram because she tries so hard. She and Grim are old and out of it — they're my grandparents, my mother's people — but they're okay most of the time. Grim still has this way of looking at me sideways, like he can't believe his poor dead daughter gave birth to this huge beast of a boy. Monster Max, the thing in the cellar. But mostly he's a pretty neat old dude, if you don't mind hearing stories about the war for the umpteenth time, and how when he was a lad the grass was greener and the air was cleaner and nobody wore T-shirts with rude words on them.

No bad T-shirts back then, I say, just those yellow stars they pinned on six million people who got sent to the gas chambers. And he'll shake his head and say I give up, the boy reads too many books. Like he's been testing me and I passed. Because once upon a time I couldn't read worth beans, and like he says my brain is now this big sponge that soaks stuff up, and he's still kind of surprised I'm not as stupid as I used to be.

Of course, if Grim knew I'd been messing around with a gang-banger, he'd figure I really *was* retarded after all.

The next time I see Worm is on the bus. Normally I walk home from school, but that day the whole junior high went on this field trip to the Museum of Science, where they've got a lot of neat stuff like a giant see-through model of the human intestine, and robots that talk like R2D2, and this really excellent planetarium where they can make the stars look like dragons breathing fire in the sky.

The bus is super crowded, so I never notice Worm until we're almost home. She's all scrunched up in one of the seats way down in the back, reading this paperback book. A thick one, too. All around her the other kids are going mental and making faces out the window and yelling goony stuff, but she never takes her nose out of that book.

When the bus driver finally comes to her stop he opens the door and waits, like he knows what happens next. The really strange thing is, Worm gets up from her seat but she never stops reading. She walks down the aisle with the book up close to her eyes and she doesn't look anywhere else, not even at her feet to see where she's going. Like nothing is going to stop her reading, not even for as long as it takes to get off the bus.

She keeps reading even when some of the other kids make fun of her. "*Book*worm, *book*worm, ugly little *book*worm."

Worm acts like she doesn't even hear them. As far as she's concerned she's not even there, she's walking inside her book and nobody can touch her.

Because of what happened when I saved her miner's helmet, I'm figuring she'll at least glance at me when she goes by, but she doesn't even notice me. Which if you know how big I am is like not noticing an elephant in your living room.

Weird. Definitely weird.

Even when she's off the bus she doesn't stop reading. She walks away from the bus stop, heading for the crummy end of town, but she never takes her nose out of that book.

"Hey, Frankenstein, what are you looking at?"

"Nothing," I say, but everybody laughs.

They go: "Max and Bookworm sitting in a tree, K-I-S-S-I-N-G!"

But they're wrong, because I'm not going gooey for any girl.

No way.

4.

You Know Who

The next day I'm hanging around the park. It's not much of a park. Just this sloping-down grass place by the old millpond, with a statue of a guy on a horse. Some Civil War general, and he's pointing his sword at the pond like he's going to chase the ducks away. The whole statue is this rusted green color except for his hat, which is white where the birds are always crapping on it.

I'm sitting on this bench by the edge of the pond, tossing pebbles into the water and thinking it's a good thing it's Saturday, because it's way too nice for school. Sometimes I like to stare at the way the sun glitters on the water, these jagged bits of light that float like diamonds or something, and if you look at it long enough you feel sort of hypnotized. Like somebody has cast a spell and when you wake up the world will be changed into a better place.

So I'm sitting there kind of zoned and not really thinking about anything when a familiar voice says, "I heard they call you Freak the Mighty."

I look around and there she is. The Bookworm. Sitting on the bench and staring at me with these really intense green eyes. Eyes so hot and bright you can almost feel the heat.

"Freak the Mighty was two people," I tell her. "Kevin and me."

"Who's Kevin?" she asks.

And so I tell her about my best friend Kevin Avery, a three-foot-high kid with a brain like Einstein, and how the other kids called him Freak because he had leg braces and this crummy disease that meant he couldn't grow. How I used to act so dumb that everyone, including me, thought I didn't have a brain, until Kevin showed me how to think. And how the two of us became Freak the Mighty and went on a lot of cool adventures, slaying dragons and fools and walking high above the world.

"Cool," she says. "So where is he now, your little friend Kevin? Did he move away or something?"

I don't really want to talk about it, but there's something about the way Worm listens that makes it okay. "He died," I tell her. "Last year."

She just sits there for a while, thinking about it. Then she goes, "What a crummy deal."

"Yeah," I say. "It was."

"So," she goes, "now you're Max the Mighty."

For some reason that makes my ears burn hot. "I'm just Max," I tell her. "Just plain Max."

Worm has this sort of smile on her face, like she knows a secret about me, and she's about to say what it is when a worried voice calls out.

"Rachel! Leave the nice man alone!"

I turn and see this woman perched on a bench nearby. She looks real nervous, like she's going to leap up any second and scream for the cops. Like because I'm big and goofy looking I might be a pervert or something.

But before I can get really steamed up I notice the woman looks familiar. She looks a lot like Worm, only older and sadder.

"Rachel!" the woman says.

Worm goes, "It's okay, Mom. He's from school."

The woman gets up from the bench and comes over. She's wearing this long, old-fashioned black dress and she's got this stiff-legged way of walking, like her feet are hurting and she doesn't want them to touch the ground.

When she gets closer I notice these dark bruises under her eyes, and right away I know there's something scaring her and it's not just me.

"I'm sorry, sir," she says, in a low sweet voice that's even sadder than her eyes. "I thought you were a stranger."

She's calling me "sir" like I'm a grown-up, and that makes me feel a little weird. I sort of like it and don't like it at the same time. The trouble with

14

looking like a grown-up is the older I get the more I look like my father. Looking like your father is okay unless dear old Dad happens to be Killer Kane and he's in prison for murdering your mother. Which means people look at me and think maybe I'll grow up to be just like him, or worse.

Worm goes, "We'll be safe here, Mom."

She thinks because I got the gang-banger to leave her alone I can make her safe all the time. What a joke. If she knew what a sapsucker I really am she'd get a head start and never stop running.

"Safe?" I ask. "Safe from what?"

"Never mind that, Rachel," her mom says. "We mustn't involve this young man in our troubles."

But her mom sits down, too. The three of us together on the bench like we're waiting for a bus. Which is sort of strange but okay.

It's quiet for a while, and then Worm pipes up, "You know what that pond reminds me of? *The Wind in the Willows.* Remember how Daddy used to read me that story?"

"I remember," her mom says, kind of wistful.

Worm roots around inside her backpack until she finds a dog-eared copy of the book. She flips through the pages but you can tell she's practically got the thing memorized, she's read it so many times. "Remember how Mole and Badger and Rat like to row around in their little boat? And Mr. Toad is always acting so grand and getting into trouble?" Her voice is going higher, like

15

talking about the story is making her feel like a little kid again. She turns to me and says, "Remember?"

"Um . . . not exactly," I say.

"You never read *The Wind in the Willows*?"

I go, "Um, I saw the cartoon version. On TV." Which sounds so lame, having to admit you never read a really famous book.

I'm expecting Worm to give me a hard time, but she doesn't. Instead she says, "We don't even *have* a TV. You Know Who won't let us."

"Huh?" I say.

"My creepy stepfather. He hates TV even more than he hates books. My real dad loves TV *and* books."

"Rachel!" her mom says, like a warning.

"Well, he does," Worm insists. "My real dad is always sending me stuff to read. He calls me his little bookworm."

Her mom stands up and takes a deep breath. "Come along," she says, taking Worm by the hand. "We have to keep moving."

I'm wondering why they have to keep moving when suddenly this old black station wagon screeches to a halt in the street behind us. No, not a station wagon exactly, it's an old Cadillac hearse, the kind that isn't used for funerals anymore. The motor is smoking and drippy streaks of rust make it look like the hearse is bleeding from the inside.

Suddenly the door flies open and out pops this tall skinny dude with a floppy black hat and a long black coat and black shoes — everything black.

It's the Undertaker. And he's coming to get us.

5.

The Undertaker

They call him the Undertaker because he dresses in black and drives this ratty old hearse. I've seen him on street corners and downtown, waving this Bible around and telling people to give him money because he knows the Truth with a capital "T." Only he never quotes from the Good Book like a real preacher, he just acts like he'll thump you on the head if you don't fork over some cash.

Some people like to egg him on and get him really shouting, but I always steer clear. He is just another angry nutbar ranting about the world gone wrong. A street crazy with a mean streak.

You see a guy like that, you never think he might have a wife and child at home.

"Don't you run from me!" he's shouting. Only he's the one doing the running. Coming right at us, waving his arms. With the long black coat and his cold dark eyes he looks like some kind of crazy black bird flapping his wings.

"Run from me and you run from the Lord!" he snarls.

He's staring furious hard at Worm's mom. She's not looking at him, or me, or even at her daughter. She's looking straight down at the ground like she hopes it will open up and swallow her.

"You hear me?" the man in black shouts. "You hear!?"

"I wasn't running," she explains in this strange dead voice. "We just went for a walk."

I look over at Worm. She's kind of curled up on the bench, hugging her knees. Her eyes are open but you can tell she's not seeing anything on the outside.

I reach out to tap her on the shoulder, to get her attention, and that's when the man in black screams: *"Don't touch that girl!"* Spit flies out of his mouth, he's so angry. His face is white and tight, like a skull without enough skin. "Rachel! Get away from that man this instant!"

Worm won't look at me. She moves slow-footed to where her mom waits.

The Undertaker has planted himself in front of me, like a stake driven into the ground. "What did they tell you?" he demands. "Speak to me, you big oaf!"

I don't know what to say so I decide to stand up instead. The man in black watches me get a lot bigger and taller than he is, and he takes a few steps back, like he doesn't want my shadow to touch him.

I'm still trying to think of what to do next when Worm's mother comes to life. "You win, Martin," she says to the man in black. "Come along, Rachel. Let's go home."

Worm follows her mom to the old hearse. Then just before she gets inside she breaks away and runs back to me and grabs hold of my jacket.

"Rachel! Get back here!"

Worm whispers, "Don't forget," and then she turns and runs back to the hearse. A moment later they speed away, tires screeching.

I'm standing there like the biggest dork in the world when I realize that Worm hid something in my jacket pocket.

6.

Run for Your Life

The lump in my pocket is a book. *The Wind in the Willows*, the worn-out old copy Worm had in her backpack. I open up the cover and see where she's written her name and address on the inside, with the instructions RETURN OR ELSE.

Don't forget. So that's what she meant.

Just my luck. I'm sitting on a park bench minding my own business and now I'm supposed to return a book to a weird girl who's in trouble. I figure that's why Worm put the book in my pocket, so I'd follow her home and be Max the Mighty and save her from her creepy stepdad and leap over tall buildings in a single bound like Superman.

Yeah right.

But even though I'm a weenie, something way inside thinks maybe I *should* return the book and make sure Worm and her mom are okay. That's when my brain says, *Don't be a doughnut — you want to return the book, put it in the mail.*

But the rest of me is thinking I've got to do something, even if it scares me.

Because the Undertaker is always spouting about punishing sinners, and how only he knows what is true, the Truth with a capital "T." What a load of baloney. A man who'd do that to his own family, treat them like dirtballs, he wouldn't know the truth if it bit him on the butt.

The address inside the book is in the projects. That's a place where people don't have enough money, and half the stuff that should be inside the houses is left outside, like old baby strollers, and busted furniture, and cheesy toys that always look sad in the rain. The wrong side of the tracks, like Gram says, except they took out the railroad tracks before I was born, so now it's just the wrong side of town.

Anyhow, I'm trudging along, looking out for cracks in the sidewalk because now I need good luck more than ever. And the more I think about how the Undertaker treats his family, the more it burns me. Cracking his voice like a whip and talking to Worm like she was nothing special, just a thing to be yelled at.

Part of me wants to stop and go back to the millpond and forget about the girl and her mom, but I keep going. Like my brain has switched off and I'm this lumbering beast with feet as big as shoe boxes.

After a while I get to her neighborhood. The buildings kind of lean the wrong way and the shadows are long and spooky. The street signs have been torn down or sprayed over, and I'm trying to figure out which way to go when the shouting starts.

The Undertaker and Rachel's mom. The woman's voice is high and sharp and angry, but you can tell she's scared, too. The Undertaker, well, it makes me feel kind of sick in my stomach because he sounds so cruel and hateful.

I'm like a dinosaur with a second brain in its tail, except the extra brain is in my feet and they're making me follow the terrible dark noise. Follow it through the gloomy shadows that live in the alley, and past the filled-to-the-brim Dumpster, and around by the rusty chain-link fence.

It's still daytime, but the old buildings are so close together it might as well be night. I keep on going and the whole time I've got this feeling like I'm on an elevator going down too fast but I can't get off and any second it's going to hit bottom.

The angry voices are getting louder.

"Keep your hands off that child!"

"Shut up, woman! Shut your mouth or I'll break it!"

"Leave her alone or I'll call the police! And this time I'll tell them the truth!"

They're fighting about the Worm, I can feel that

in my bones. And then I come around the corner of the old tenement building and see the old hearse parked in the street. There's a light coming from the basement apartment. The kind of apartment where the entrance is under the front stoop and there's iron bars on the windows.

The Undertaker is shouting, "I will punish that child as the Lord sees fit!"

And then her mother goes, "You've never even read that Bible! You're not a real preacher, you're a fake!"

And then *smack* comes the noise of a hand slapping hard against a face and then the sound of a woman sobbing. "This can't go on," the woman whimpers. "Martin, please stop. Don't do it, please."

"Quit your blubbering!"

But the woman keeps crying. Crying from deep inside, like her world has cracked open and all the good is leaking out. It's a sound I remember from a long, long time ago, when my father made my own mother cry, and that's why my feet won't let me run away.

I'm not really thinking about what happens next but I want to stop that terrible sad crying and that's why I go down the steps to the front door. Thinking maybe if I ring the bell they'll stop fighting. Dingdong and everything gets better. But there isn't any doorbell and before I can make a fist and knock, the woman cries out, "No! No!"

and then something falls to the floor and everything gets very quiet.

The silence makes me wish I was a thousand miles away. And when I look into the room through the bars on the window, I see a terrible thing. A thing so horrible it feels like my heart has stuck to my ribs and won't ever beat again.

Rachel's mom is lying on the floor, blocking a bedroom door with her body. Her eyes are black and bruised and her nose is bloody and she's not moving.

The Undertaker yanks her arms and pulls her away from the door. He's about to open it. There's a cruel look on his pale white face, and his eyes are cold and gleaming and his angry hands are reaching out.

Ker-wham!

That's when I come crashing through the front door and knock it off the hinges and slam it flat on the floor.

"You!" he screams. But he sees the look in my eyes and how big I am and he backs away.

Rachel's mom moans and raises her head and when she sees me through her swollen eyes she almost smiles.

"Get away from that door!" the Undertaker shouts.

That makes me want to open the door, and I do.

The first thing I see is a light shining on a book. Worm is sitting in a corner with her knees up, in the dark. She's got the old miner's helmet on her head and the light is aimed at this book she's reading.

She knows I'm there but she won't look at me. She's all shut up inside.

When I get my mouth working, it says, "Come on. You have to get out of here. We have to call the police."

Worm just keeps reading her book like the book will save her. Like her stepfather can't touch her as long as her miner's light is shining.

But that won't stop him. Nothing will stop him except getting her away from him, so I grab her backpack, scoop her up in my arms and carry her out of the room.

When I get clear of her bedroom the Undertaker takes a run at me, then pulls up. "She's mine!" he screams. "Give her to me!"

I decide I'd rather die than do what he wants.

Rachel's mom has crawled up from the floor. It's hard for her to talk, but she looks at me and says, "You've got to get her away from here. Please. Take her away!"

Worm has her face hard against my chest and she won't look at her mother.

"Run away!" her mother urges. "Do it! Go!"

And that's how I became a desperate criminal and kidnapper, wanted by the law.

7.
Heading for Home

When you get in trouble, head for home. That's the first thing that comes into my head after me and Worm get clear of the alley. The Undertaker doesn't follow us, which sort of surprises me. Somebody takes away his stepdaughter and he just lets her go?

Of course he's got his hands full, after what he did to his poor wife.

Worm lets me carry her out of the basement apartment, but then she wants to walk on her own. When I ask if she's okay, she doesn't say a word but she reaches out and takes my hand.

"Grim and Gram will know what to do," I promise her.

We can hear sirens wee-ooing in the distance and I'm thinking they'll be putting the cuffs on the Undertaker so he can't hurt anybody else. I don't even want to think about what will happen to Worm, or what she should do until he's locked up in jail and can't hurt her anymore.

We're cutting across the backyards, heading for home because Gram will make everything okay somehow. Hey, after dealing with a big doughnut brain like me, helping an eleven-year-old girl should be easy, right?

Wrong, because when we come up to the back of the house, there are blue lights flashing through the windows. Cop cars in the street. Something in my brain goes "uh-oh."

I put my finger to my lips and Worm nods and doesn't make a sound.

There's a row of thick hedges that runs close to one side of the house, between our yard and the neighbors. I used to hide in there when I was little — after my mom died, but before Kevin moved next door. I'd hide myself in the hedges and pretend I was far away inside the forest where it was green and cool and the good smell of leaves and earth made me feel safe. Grim and Gram knew about the secret hedge place, but they never let on.

I'm way too big to hide in there now, but if I crouch real low and keep my head down I can still look around to the front yard without being seen. And what I see there just about blows my mind.

The Undertaker. He's with the cops but he's not in handcuffs. He's acting all weepy and upset and he's telling the police the biggest bunch of lies you ever heard.

"He was after Rachel. Menacing her! And when my wife tried to stop him, he hit her."

It never happened that way, but he sounds like he believes it. He wipes his eyes and sniffles a bit and says, "You've got to catch him and lock him away before he does my girl any harm."

The cops don't say much, except they tell the Undertaker to stay back. By now the front door has opened and Grim and Gram have come out on the steps. The blue lights make them look pale and old.

"What happened?" Gram asks, real worried. "Is it Max? Did something happen to Max?"

One of the cops says, "Is your grandson home, ma'am? We'd like a word with him."

The Undertaker hears that and goes nuts. "A word!" he shouts. "The boy assaulted my wife and ran off with our girl! Arrest him!"

Grim kind of staggers and grabs hold of Gram and then they're holding each other up and looking sick. Grim says, "Impossible! There must be some kind of mistake. Max wouldn't hurt a soul."

The other cop pipes up and says, "Maybe he doesn't know his own strength, sir. Have you seen him in the last few hours?"

Gram's voice is shaking. "He went down to the millpond," she says. "To the park. He goes there almost every day."

The Undertaker charges up behind the cops, waving his hat around. "See!" he shouts. "I told you! He followed us home from the park! Just like I said!"

Grim straightens up and goes, "You'd better tell us what happened, officer."

The cop doesn't look too happy about it, but he clears his throat and goes, "This man says a youth fitting Maxwell's description broke into their apartment and ran off with an eleven-year-old girl. While trying to stop him, the girl's mother received several blows to the face."

"And the woman told you Max attacked her?" Grim asks.

"She agrees with her husband," the cop says with a shrug.

Grim's voice gets stronger. "Then it wasn't our Max. Couldn't have been."

The other cop goes, "I'm afraid Maxwell was seen leaving the scene of the crime, carrying the girl. There's really nobody else who fits the description, sir. I mean, a boy that big. The door was broken down, knocked right off the hinges."

Gram has a quiet kind of voice but I hear her clear as a bell. "Listen to me, you people. There has been a mistake. Max will be home any minute, and he can explain for himself."

Inside I'm going, *Good for you, Gram*. And I'm thinking maybe I should come out and tell everybody what really happened, and how the

Undertaker is a total liar. Why shouldn't they believe me instead of him?

Then Gram says something that makes my heart drop down into my shoes.

"It wasn't Max who broke down the door and kidnapped the girl," Gram says. "Our boy would never do such a thing. I assume you're taking fingerprints?"

The cops both nod.

"Good," says Gram, like everything is settled. "That will prove it isn't our grandson."

Fingerprints. Mine will be all over the door I busted down. And besides, I really did break in and run off with Worm. That part is true.

The Undertaker is wiping his eyes with his floppy black hat. "Poor Rachel," he sobs. "My little girl."

"We'll find her," one of the cops tells him. "Maxwell Kane is too big to hide."

The other cop pats him on the back and says, "You'll get your daughter back. I promise."

Worm moans and goes, "I knew it. Nobody can stop him."

That's when I decide there's only one right thing to do.

Run away with Worm to a place where the Undertaker can't find her.

8.
Maxwell Kane Is Too Big to Hide

The last time I ran away from home I was five years old and took my teddy bear along for company. Now I'm fourteen and I've got a real live eleven-year-old girl hanging on to my hand like she's afraid I'll disappear.

We're cutting through the backstreets, away from the flashing blue lights, trying to stay out of sight.

"I knew that would happen," Worm says. "He can make my mom say anything. It happened before. They were fighting, you know, like tonight? And somebody called the cops. But when the cops got there, my mom said it was all her fault."

"So what do we do now?" I ask.

"I want to find my real dad," Worm announces. "He'll know what to do."

Actually, that makes sense. Let him be the one

to protect her, he's probably a whole lot braver and smarter than I am.

I go, "So where's your real dad? Does he live nearby?"

Worm shakes her head. "Montana," she says. "In a place called Chivalry."

Great. Wonderful. Geography isn't my best subject, but I know Montana is at least a thousand miles from here, maybe more. So whatever hope it gave me, that all comes crashing down.

"You could phone him," I say.

But Worm shakes her head. "He hasn't got a phone. I've got to see him, okay? It's important." She sounds like she's holding back tears.

I go, "Okay, okay. Take it easy. We'll find your dad, I promise."

The truth of it is, I feel like crying, too. Running out on Grim and Gram is about the worst thing I've ever done. It makes me feel like there's mice fighting inside my stomach and butterflies flitting around inside my head. Maybe I really am stupid, but I can't see anything else to do but somehow get all the way to Montana and let Worm's father fix everything.

More than anything I wish my friend Kevin were here — he'd have a plan. A really cool plan with lots of adventure in it.

"We could take a bus," Worm says. "Buses go to Montana, right?"

"I guess so."

I'm thinking she could go on her own, she doesn't need me to ride on a bus, right? And then I think: What would Kevin do if he were here? He'd figure she was a damsel in distress, and it was our job to keep her safe. No problemo, he'd say. Freak the Mighty to the rescue. All for one and one for all.

Except now it's just me.

"Please?" Worm says.

"Okay, we'll take a bus to Montana and find your real dad."

Thinking about going that far from home makes me kind of sick and dizzy and excited all at the same time. Also I'm wishing the sun would hurry up and go down because something that cop said bothers me. *Maxwell Kane is too big to hide.* And he's right, it's not like I can blend in, or shrink myself down to normal size. All they have to do is be on the lookout for a moon-faced goon with size seventeen shoes. Besides, just about everybody in town knows me by sight.

So we're stumbling along, with me nervous and worried and not paying attention to where I'm going, and that's when I crash right into the trash can. *Wham!* Stuff flies all over the street. Bottles and garbage and old newspapers and a ratty bundle of clothes.

"Wait a minute," Worm says, checking out the old clothes. She picks out a suit coat with holes in the elbows, and an old tie with stripes, and one of those hats like gangsters wear in the movies.

"This is exactly what you need," she says, her eyes going bright. "A disguise."

Ten minutes later we're heading for the bus station. I'm wearing the old suit coat and a fat tie like Grim wears to church on Sunday and a gangster hat pulled down so the brim hides part of my big fat face.

Worm has the idea to smear my cheeks with dirt so it looks like whiskers.

"There you are," she says, dusting the dirt from her hands. "All grown-up."

"No way."

"This'll work," she insists. "I read it in *The Adventures of Huckleberry Finn*. When Huck got in really bad trouble he'd put on a disguise. One time he had to dress up like a girl. You can pretend to be an adult."

"I guess." Already I'm getting the idea that it's easier to go along with her than argue. But I look about as much like a grown-up as a brontosaurus butt.

"We'll need money," Worm reminds me.

I've still got the twenty dollars Grim gave me for my birthday, stuck in the secret compartment in my wallet, and Worm has five dollars in a plastic purse in her backpack, and we figure that'll buy us tickets as far as the next state at least. I'm not thinking about what happens after that, or how we'll really get to Montana, which might as well be as far away as the moon. I'm mostly worried about what happens right now, this very minute.

We're a block from the bus station when the Worm goes, "Uh-oh."

She's spotted a cop car coming into the town square. No lights flashing, but they head straight for the bus station like they're expecting to find us there.

Of course. The first place they'd look, right? And I'm heading right for it.

What a moron.

The cops get out of the car and go to the ticket window. So in another minute they'll figure out we haven't got there yet, and they'll wait to grab us.

Maxwell Kane is too big to hide.

What he really meant was, Maxwell Kane is too stupid to get away.

Maybe they're right and I really am a doughnut brain. And then again, maybe I'm not.

"This way," I whisper to Worm.

We cut away from the town square, down the alleys that go by the big warehouses, out to the place where the interstate highway ramp heads west.

"What are we going to do?" Worm wants to know.

"We're going to break the law," I tell her. And then I do something I promised Gram I'd never do.

I stick out my thumb to hitch us a ride.

9.

The Prairie Schooner

There's nothing colder than wind on the highway. The gusts kick up from cars and trucks that zoom by like we're invisible. Drivers looking straight ahead, making sure their eyes don't see us.

I'm thinking this is a really stupid idea, trying to hitch a ride, when Worm nudges me and says, "You can go home now if you want."

I go, "Huh?"

She won't look at me because her eyes are red and she doesn't want me to see her crying. "It isn't fair, making you come with me. I'm the one who has to run away from You Know Who."

She means her stepfather, with all his lies about what really happened to her mom, and what he might do to Worm if she stays. My brain hears her talking and goes, *Do it, doughnut head. Go home. Tell the truth and see what happens*.

My brain is really stupid sometimes, because

only a crudball creep would leave an eleven-year-old girl all alone in the world, running away from a bad-news dude like the Undertaker. Besides, once we find her real father he can take over and make things right, so it's not like I'm running away forever.

That's what I tell myself, and I'm trying real hard to believe it.

Guys who brag about how cool it is to hitchhike are a bunch of liars. In the first place, you have to stand there like roadkill while dirt blows up in your face. Also your feet ache and your nose fills with the stink of smelly motors and hot tires, and you keep smiling and waving your stupid thumb but nobody stops.

Worm is fidgeting around and acting worried. Her face is so pale you could count every freckle, and her eyes look nervous and scared.

"You got a book in there, right?" I say, pointing at her backpack. "Go ahead and read it. Let me worry about getting a ride."

It's like she was waiting for permission. About two seconds later she's got her nose in a book called *A Wrinkle in Time*. You'd think she was in a library instead of hanging around beside a highway. You can tell she's really good at reading no matter where she is or what's happening around her. There's this look on her face like she's not there at all, she's gone wherever the book takes her.

Me, every time a truck goes by and smacks me in the face with a gust of stinky wind, it makes me feel dumber and dumber. Great idea, hitching a ride. Right up there with making firecrackers in the basement, or that time I put orange soda in the goldfish bowl so the fish could have a drink.

Finally I get so desperate, I decide to try praying, even though it's probably against the rules.

Dear Lord, I'm praying, *if You'll just make somebody stop and pick us up, I promise to be good and pray for more important things, like ending wars and feeding all the hungry people and saving the planet and stuff. Your immediate servant, Maxwell T. Kane.*

It probably doesn't count as a miracle, but when I open my eyes, this old school bus is pulling over into the breakdown lane, kicking up a cloud of dust.

"Hey, cool!" Worm says, looking up from her book.

When the dust clears I see it isn't a school bus exactly. Like maybe it used to be a school bus until somebody painted it over with splotches of bright colors. Ziggy stripes of yellow and zaggy patches of pink and another color that looks like the inside of a ripe cantaloupe. It has curtains on the windows and a big chrome air horn and a name in drippy purple paint on the side:

THE PRAIRIE SCHOONER

I figure anybody who'd paint an old bus like that is probably insane, or at least dangerously wacko. I'm going to tell Worm to forget it, we'll wait for another ride, but it's too late, she's already running for the door.

I catch up with her just as she's scrambling up the steps into the bus. "Hang on!" I'm panting. "Wait a sec!"

I look up to where the driver sits. He's this old dude with silvery white hair braided into long pigtails and a huge lumpy nose and not much chin. He's got a big wide smile and a Santa Claus fat belly, and he's wearing a Hawaiian shirt that hurts my eyes, it's that bright. But the strangest thing of all is his eyeglasses. The lenses are as big around as coffee cups, and so thick his eyes look like they're coming at you through telescopes.

"Howdy doody!" the old dude says. "Welcome aboard. Have a seat and rest your feet!"

The door whacks shut behind me and we're moving. He hits the horn and the loud noise almost stops my heart. I'm staggering, trying to hold on as the bus speeds up and Worm is looking around and going, "I guess you live here, huh?"

"Home sweet home!" the driver says, and gives his horn another blast.

The inside of the bus does look like home, in a funny way.

The old passenger seats have been ripped out and in the front part of the bus there's a couple of old couches bolted to the floor. In the back is a stove and a sink and one of those little refrigerators, and beyond that a couple of bunk beds built against the wall.

I'm trying to take it all in and keep my balance at the same time. Meanwhile Worm settles down on the old couch and acts like everything is normal.

The bus swerves and I fall onto the couch, next to Worm. The driver hits the horn again and shouts, "Make way! Coming through!" Then he's looking at me in the rearview mirror, and he says, "I'm the Dippy Hippie, pleased to meet you!"

I go, "Huh?"

"They call me the Dippy Hippie," he explains. "Dip for short."

I'm thinking maybe we should use made-up names, but before I can think of any, Worm looks up from her book and goes, "I'm Rachel and this is Max the Mighty."

"Rachel and Max," Dip says. "Groovy!"

He's got both hands on the big steering wheel and he's keeping the bus square in the middle of the slow lane. You can tell he's a good driver, even if he is halfway blind, and there's something in his voice that makes me think maybe he's not so strange after all.

"Where you folks headed?" he asks. "Anyplace special?"

"Um," I say, because I'm not sure if it's a secret or not.

"Chivalry," Worm pipes up. "That's in Montana."

"Montana, huh?" Dip nods to himself. "I'm headed in that general direction, more or less. We'll see where the highway takes us. Make yourselves at home. If you're hungry, there's food in the refrigerator. Help yourself."

Food sounds good, so I make me and the Worm a couple of bologna sandwiches with plenty of mustard. I've got no problem finishing mine, but before Worm gets halfway done her head is nodding and her eyelids are fluttering and then she kind of slumps over against me, fast asleep.

She's hugging *A Wrinkle in Time* to her chest and breathing deep and quiet and she looks so peaceful it makes me feel sleepy, too.

The next thing I know the bus has stopped moving and it's dark out.

"Rest stop," a voice explains softly. "All that snoring back there, I figured I'd better catch a few winks before I nodded off at the wheel."

Dip is lying on the other couch. He's got his hands behind his head and I can't tell where he's looking because there's no lights on, just a few stars shining in through the windshield.

"You want to tell me about it?" he asks, real quiet.

I don't know what to say, so I make up some lame story about how we missed the Greyhound bus and decided to try hitching a ride.

"Uh-huh," Dip says. "Rachel is your sister, is that it?"

"Not exactly," I say.

He doesn't say anything for a while and then he sits up and I can see him looking at us. Looking at how the Worm is sleeping so sound and comfortable on that old couch. Like she was safe in her own home. Dip nods to himself and then he says, "Fact is, I'm grateful for the company. Big bus like this doesn't feel right empty."

"It's real nice," I say, looking around. And it is nice, even if it's old and sort of shabby.

"I'm a retired schoolteacher," Dip says. "Me and the wife been planning to take off and see the world, like we always dreamed of doing but never had the time. Then she passed away all of a sudden. Kind of caught me by surprise, you know? After a while I got tired of feeling sorry for myself, so I finished fixing up the Prairie Schooner and took off. You know what a prairie schooner is, Max?"

"No," I say.

Dip sits up straighter and his voice gets happy again. He tells me how in the old days when the settlers headed out West, some of them rigged sails on their wagons and let the wind blow them onto the prairies. Sailing through fields of green, green grass under a big blue sky and all their lives in front of them, until they found a place and made it home.

"Is that where you're headed?" I ask. "Out to the prairies?"

"Wherever the wind takes me," he says. "That's where I'm going. How's that sound to you?"

"It sounds just fine," I say.

10.
Maxwell vs. the Ants

After resting his eyes for a while, Dip gets back behind the wheel and keeps on driving for hours and hours. Through the windshield the highway looks like a long dark tunnel with a white line disappearing into the darkness. Like we're flying forward in a funny kind of spaceship, and the stars are fireflies in outer space, lighting our way.

I ask Dip where we're going, exactly.

"We're heading for the horizon," he says. "Never look back. Eyes on the future, Max. That's the way to go."

Yeah right. Except when the future is a prison cell.

Worm keeps snoozing, so fast and deep asleep you could set off a cherry bomb and not wake her. I can tell she's dreaming, because sometimes her feet will twitch like she's running and her freckled face looks all squinted up and serious, and she's hanging on to her book so hard it'd take a crowbar to pry it out of her hands.

I got a pretty good idea what she's dreaming about. That no-good lying creep she calls You Know Who.

Sitting there in the dark with the sound of the tires taking us farther and farther away, I'm feeling pretty sorry for myself. Wishing I'd never met the girl called Worm. Because if I didn't know her, I'd probably be hanging out in the down under right this minute, reading my comic books or just lying there thinking about nothing at all. I wouldn't know any of the bad stuff that happened, or if I did, it would just be something I saw in the newspaper, or heard about from Grim and Gram.

But the truth is, I did rescue her crummy old miner's helmet and that made her think I was Max the Mighty. And I did kick down that door and help her get away. So now I'm wanted for assault and kidnapping, and nobody is going to believe me, or a strange red-haired girl who lives inside her books.

"Penny for your thoughts," Dip says. His big magnified eyes are looking at me in the rearview mirror.

"Nothin'," I say. "Just stuff."

Dip keeps that old bus heading into the west until the sun rises behind us, and I never do fall back asleep. My nerves keep sparking and twitching under my skin, like I drank too much of Grim's coffee, or stuffed myself with chocolate bars.

There's a thin kind of light in the sky that reminds me of skim milk, and the clouds look dirty and ragged where the wind is pulling them apart. When all the stars are gone, Dip slaps his hands on the wheel and says, "Anybody feel like breakfast?"

Worm pops up like somebody turned her switch on. "I'm hungry," she says, rubbing her stomach. "So hungry I could eat a house!"

"You mean a horse," I say.

"Ick," she says. "What a disgusting idea."

Then Worm gives me a big "gotcha" smile that makes me wish I'd never thought about how it would be if I'd minded my own business and thrown her stupid book away. She's the one who should be feeling sorry for herself and instead she's trying to make me laugh.

Dip pulls into a rest area and finds a spot way in back, where the tall pine trees hide us from the highway. It's green and thick and real overgrown. Like we're out in the wilderness somewhere, beyond where the road ends.

If I didn't know better I'd think we were all alone.

Dip gets out from behind the wheel real slow, and then he has to stretch and unwind, he says, because his old bones are creaky. "I'm like a rusty door hinge," he says. "Nothing a little tai chi won't fix."

"Tai chi," I say. "Is that what we're having for breakfast?"

It turns out tai chi is this strange-looking exercise Dip does each morning. Sort of like a slow-motion dance he learned from this Chinese guy. First thing Dip does is face the rising sun and bow at the waist, like he's meeting the queen or something. Then he raises up his arms real slow and he turns in a circle, holding his hands out like he's looking through a camera. Next he lifts his right leg and kind of dips down and around like he's going to tie himself in a big knot, except he changes his mind and unties himself real slow, and goes around the other way.

Remember, he's a fat guy in a killer Hawaiian shirt with long white hair done up in funny-looking pigtails. And a humongous nose and eyes that look like they're coming at you out of telescopes.

At first I want to laugh because it seems so funny, a guy like him doing this ancient Chinese dance. But there's something so cool and quiet about the way he's moving, so smooth and clean, that you have to take him seriously. He's holding out his hands and bringing them slowly around like they're the moon and he's the earth. And you can tell he's relaxed and peaceful inside.

You'd never think an old guy like Dip could move so beautiful.

Then I look over and what do you know, there's Worm copying him. She's holding out her hands just like he is, and she's got one foot up, turning slowly around. Her eyes are closed tight and there's this serious kind of look on her face that could almost be a sad kind of smile. The sun makes her red hair look glowy like the dawn, and she seems so quiet and easy with herself she almost looks like a different person, except for the freckles.

After he finishes his Chinese dance, Dip puts together the best breakfast ever. He brings out his little camp stove and sets it on a picnic table and cooks up a whole package of bacon, real slow. So slow my stomach is going nuts by the time he stirs in the scrambled eggs. He's got this brown bread that comes out of a can and he toasts that in the other fry pan and slathers it with butter.

The deal is, you put a chunk of egg and bacon on the bread and eat it that way, so you don't have to dirty any plates.

"You guys know the secret ingredient?" Dip asks.

Me and Worm, we're both chomping down so much all we can do is shake our heads.

"Fresh air," he says. "Fresh air is better than ketchup. Makes your taste buds tingle."

When he sees how hungry I am, Dip opens another can of brown bread, and by the time I put that away, my stomach feels as tight as a drum. Tight but good.

I'm feeling so full I decide to lay down on the grass and just stretch out.

Dumbo idea.

The hot feeling starts around my ankles, and before I have time to sit up, my butt is on fire.

"Help!" I cry. "I'm burning up! Help!"

I'm leaping and thrashing around like a total lunatic, ripping at my clothes.

"Fire ants!" yells Dip. "Rachel, you better get in the bus!"

The reason he wants her to go into the bus is so she won't see me pulling my pants down and dragging my butt across the grass.

I must look like the gooniest goon in the world, but I don't care. All I care about is getting rid of those fire ants.

Most people would die laughing, seeing a huge guy like me drag his bare butt in the grass while he's yipping like a poodle, but Dip, he never cracks a smile. He takes charge and shows me how to shake out my pants and brush off the fire ants, and then he turns around and pretends to study the trees while I get dressed.

It's not until we're all back in the Prairie Schooner that he lets it out. Then all of a sudden he's laughing so hard it sounds like a volcano erupting. His glasses fall off and his nose starts to run and he can't hardly breathe, and just watching him gets me laughing, too.

That finally kicks Worm off, and pretty soon

she's giggling and then laughing and pointing at me and making stupid goony faces and going, "Help! Help! My butt's on fire!" and that makes me laugh even harder.

That's when the cops come, when we're all laughing like total maniacs.

11.
The Man with the Crutch

I figure they'll handcuff me for sure. My stomach kind of sinks into my shoes and I'm just sitting there like a mental moron when Dip opens the door and goes, "Hello, officers. What's the trouble?"

One of the cops stays inside the cruiser. The other cop, a skinny dude with small dark eyes and a little mustache, he gets out and saunters over. He's got his hand on his gun and he's looking at the bus real careful.

"Please step out of the vehicle," he calls up to Dip.

Dip gives us a wink and then he gets out of the bus. Meanwhile Worm has got her nose in her book like nothing is happening, like the cops aren't there at all.

"Be glad to oblige," Dip says to the cop.

He's got his wallet chained to his pants and he pulls it out and shows the cop his driver's license. The cop studies it for a long time and then hands it back.

"We had a report of a car being hijacked," the cop says. "Have you seen any suspicious activity at the rest stop?"

Dip shakes his head and says, "No, sir. We've had the place to ourselves."

"Anyone else in the vehicle, sir?"

Dip goes, "A couple of wild outlaws. Maybe you better lock 'em up."

The cop takes him seriously and starts to pull out his gun. Real quick Dip says, "Just my two grandchildren, officer. I was making a joke."

The cop gives him a look like, *What are you try-ing to pull, buddy,* and then he relaxes a little and says, "Mind if I take a look?"

Dip shrugs and goes, "Make yourself at home."

The bus creaks as the cop comes inside. He stands there blinking like he's got spots in front of his eyes and then he sees me kind of slumped down on the couch. "What's your name?" he asks.

My mouth is too dry to talk.

"That's Mike," Dip says, coming up behind the cop. "He's a little, uh, shy."

"He a retard?" the cop asks.

Right away Dip says, "We don't use that word, officer."

After that the cop pretty much ignores Dip and

me and crouches down so he's level with Worm. "And what's your name, girlie?"

Worm won't look at him and she won't say anything.

Dip butts in. "That's Sally. Sally and Mike. Keeping their old grandpa company until their mother meets us in Denver."

The cop doesn't say anything, he just stands there and squints at me real hard, like he's seen me before. I give him a goofy look and let a little drool run down from the side of my mouth, like I really am retarded. Finally the cop grunts to himself and turns away.

"We're recommending that vehicles park within sight of the highway," the cop says to Dip. "These isolated rest spots can be dangerous."

"Yes, sir," Dip says. "Have a nice day, sir."

The skinny cop gets back in the cruiser and it glides away with the lights still flashing. Dip waits until it gets back on the highway and then he turns to me. "I figured it was nobody's business, what your real names are," he says.

"Thanks."

Dip grins. "You better wipe the drool off your chin, Max. You're pretty good at playing dumb, huh?"

"I've had some practice," I say.

And that's no lie.

We're about to get back on the highway when Worm goes, "Somebody's hiding in the woods."

54

Dip puts the brakes on and goes, "What?"

"Right over there," Worm says, pointing out the window.

All I see are bushes and thick pine trees. Then I notice the branches moving like there's something in there that wants to jump out. Probably the wind.

"It's nothing," I tell Worm. "Just your imagination."

Worm makes a face and goes, "No way. I saw something."

I'm still thinking her brain is in her book when all of a sudden the bushes open up and out comes this guy leaning on a crutch. Not a real crutch, but part of a tree branch he's using to hobble along. He's got thick yellow hair that grows down almost to his eyebrows and watery blue eyes and he looks kind of oily, like he needs a shower.

Right behind him is this scrawny-but-pretty-looking woman with eyes that kind of bulge out, like she's always surprised. Her face is a little scratched up and she's wearing a flowered dress that must have gotten dirty when she fell down. She looks scared, like she's afraid something else is going to jump out of the bushes any minute.

Dip sets the brake and gets out of the bus and rushes over to help the guy on the homemade crutch. "Max," he shouts back. "Gimme a hand!"

"You stay here," I say to Worm, but she's already back in her book and pretends not to hear me.

When the woman sees me get out of the bus she kind of cringes, like she's afraid I'll hit her or something. "Don't you worry, Miss," Dip says. "The boy is a gentle giant."

The guy with the crutch is hanging on to Dip for dear life.

"Is it broken?" Dip asks.

"Don't think so," the man with the crutch says. "Just hurts like heck."

That's when I notice the woman in the flowered dress is crying. Her eyes are all dark and circled like a raccoon's and her little nose is twitching. "Frank is in so much pain," she says. "He tried to stop them."

"Stop who?" Dip asks.

"The men who robbed us," the woman says. She's got this high, quick-talking voice, like somebody is pulling a string and making the words rush out. "They took everything and then they beat up my husband."

Frank goes, "I'll be okay." But then his crutch slips and he groans.

We help them into the bus and they collapse on the couch. Dip gets an aspirin from the first aid kit and gives it to Frank with a glass of water. "Thanks, buddy," Frank says. "Sorry to trouble you."

"No trouble," Dip says. "What happened?"

What happened is Frank and his wife, Joanie, were on their way to the West Coast because

Frank had been offered this extremely important job raising money for a hospital, and they got sleepy and decided to pull in and rest until daylight. Only when they were sound asleep these three guys in ski masks ripped open the doors and yanked them out of their car and stole it and all the money they'd saved up.

"We're broke," Frank says with a shrug. "They took everything."

Joanie sticks out her chin and goes, "We'll have to start over. It won't be the first time. We'll find a place to settle, I'll get a job."

Worm puts away her book and stares at Joanie for a while, like she wants to figure her out but she can't quite do it. "The cops were here," Worm finally says to her. "Looking for you."

Joanie pulls back like somebody slapped her. "Looking for me? What are you talking about?"

Dip explains how the police were just here a few minutes ago investigating a reported car hijacking.

"No kidding," Joanie says. "The cops were here?"

Frank looks uncomfortable.

"There's a pay phone right over there," Dip says, pointing. "I'll call 911, you can file a report."

He's digging into his pocket for a quarter when Joanie grabs hold of his arm. "Please," she begs him. "Don't."

Frank, he lays back on the couch and smiles to

himself. "I'm tired of lying," he says. "These are good folks, we can tell them what really happened."

"Frank!" Joanie sounds frightened.

"I don't care," he says. "Let 'em turn me in if they want to."

Dip goes, "What are you saying?"

"It's all my fault," Frank says, real quiet. "You see, the truth is, I'm a wanted man."

12.
Safe Inside Her Book

"Oh, Frank," Joanie says. "You make it sound like you're a criminal!"

Frank, he's propped up on the couch, but he already looks better, like he can't wait to get something off his chest. "The law thinks I am. Call 911 and we'll find out. They'll bust me, guaranteed."

Joanie goes, "It's not fair!"

"Fair has nothing to do with it," Frank says. "The law deals in facts, and the facts are against us."

It turns out that Frank and Joanie worked for this orphanage that specialized in crippled kids. Frank was in charge of the staff, and this guy he hired to keep track of the money was actually stealing it and making it look like Frank signed the checks.

"The guy was smooth," Frank says. "I never knew what was going on until it was too late. I just never believed a man could be so low he'd steal from crippled orphans."

"You mean disabled," Dip reminds him. "Not crippled."

"Disabled in the crippled sense," Frank says. "Polio and leprosy and such."

Dip gets this funny look and goes, "I thought they had a cure for polio. And leprosy."

Frank waves his hand and says, "There are a few tragic exceptions, I'm afraid. It doesn't matter now. Facts are facts. The money was stolen and the orphanage was shut down. And it was my fault. I should have known better."

"I see," Dip says.

Then Frank looks Dip straight in the eye and says, "Go ahead. Make that call. I wouldn't blame you."

Dip looks at Frank and he looks at me and Worm, and you can tell he's got a lot on his mind. Finally he goes, "Live and let live, eh? What say we all forget our troubles for the moment and get back on the road?"

Frank lets out a sigh and goes, "I knew you were okay."

Joanie jumps up and gives Dip a big hug and says, "Thank you! Thank you!"

Her eyes are a little wet from holding back tears, but by the time we're back up to speed, Joanie is already making herself at home. She spots the little refrigerator and goes, "Hey, Dip! You got anything to eat? I'm starved!"

And that's how Frank and Joanie joined our little family, and helped good old Dip fill up his empty bus.

Worm goes back to her books. She's got a bunch of paperbacks in her backpack and she tells me she's done with *A Wrinkle in Time* for now and she's into these stories called The Earthsea Trilogy. They're all about sorcerers, and dragons who can talk if you know their secret language, and a lot of other cool stuff that happened a long time ago.

"Magic ruled the world," Worm says, not looking up.

Which makes me think of the times when me and Kevin turned ourselves into Freak the Mighty and we made up our own kind of magic. Once when we were walking along an ordinary street — just dull normal houses and barking dogs — Kevin had me convinced we were crossing a moat into a big castle.

Thinking about that makes me miss Kevin so bad, it hurts inside my chest, and then all of a sudden I'm missing Gram and Grim. I'm even missing my stupid bedroom with the saggy mattress. I'm missing my mom, I'm missing just about everything, even the stuff I hate.

Dip, he sees me in his rearview mirror and goes, "Hey, Max! Come on up here and keep me company."

So there I am, sitting right behind Dip and we're

seeing what comes down the road. For a while we're going through a place where there are tons of big refineries and factories alongside the highway, and a funny yellow light that makes it look like the sky is burning real slow.

"What a pit," Frank says.

But I think it looks kind of cool, like the end of the world but not quite, and Dip chimes in to say you'd be surprised how beautiful America can be, if you get away from the turnpike. That kind of kills the conversation for a while, until Joanie taps me on the shoulder and goes, "What about you, big guy? What's your story? Is the girl really your sister or what?"

I decide the best thing to do is keep my mouth shut about how we're looking for Worm's father, because the way Joanie is looking at me, so kind and curious and helpful, I'd probably tell her the truth and get us into trouble.

She goes, "The silent type, huh? You're keeping a secret, is that it? Come on, share it with Joanie."

Frank, he's stretched out on one of the couches with all of the pillows to ease the pain. "Leave him alone," he calls out. "He'll talk to us in his own good time, won't you, kid?"

Meanwhile, Dip keeps on driving. Like his hands have melted to the wheel and he can't let go even if he wanted to. He's humming a little song to himself, and it sounds like the tires humming under us and the wind that's blowing his old Prairie Schooner bus across America.

It's just a dumb little song without any words, but it makes me feel peaceful and happy, and I'm thinking there's no place I'd rather be than right here with these people. Like we're all sharing something none of us can talk about or it'll disappear. Like we really are safe and nothing can touch us.

Maybe Worm is right. Maybe there is magic in the world, if you think about it.

When the sun goes down, Worm switches on her miner's light and keeps reading.

I'm kind of dozing off, listening to the hum of the tires and that old bus engine purring along, but I'm awake enough to see Joanie settle down on the couch next to Worm.

"Must be a good story, huh?" she says.

Worm shrugs but doesn't say anything, and she won't look up from her book.

"I bet you've got a story of your own to tell," Joanie says. "You want to talk about it, just us girls?"

Worm ignores her and keeps reading.

"I'm here," Joanie says, her voice going soft. "Whenever you're ready, I'm here."

There's something in her voice that makes me not quite trust her, but I don't need to say anything to Worm. I can tell she feels the same way.

I sleep for a while, but whenever I wake up, Worm's light is still on, and she's turning pages, staying safe inside her book.

13.
There's a Sucker Born Every Minute

There's a place in Indiana where the cornfields look like a big green ocean. Everything is pretty flat except for these low, rolling hills, and when we come over the top you can see just about forever. All there is to see are miles and miles of green cornstalks, millions and millions of them. You can see the wind moving through the corn from miles away, and it looks like waves rolling in from far out at sea.

Dip lets down the windows and you can hear the air moving through the fields. This soft sighing noise like when you put a shell to your ear and hear the ocean. Only it doesn't sound like the ocean to Dip — he says it's the cheering noise from halfway around the world, of all those people who love to eat corn on the cob.

"They're cheering from Maine to Texas, can't

you hear them?" he says, cupping a hand to his big floppy ear. "They're cheering in Tokyo and Timbuktu!"

I don't believe a word of it, but Dip swears Timbuktu is a real place, and there's nothing much there, which is why they joke about it.

Of course it isn't all corn in Indiana, they grow some people, too, and every once in a while a little town springs up out of nowhere, like it crash-landed from a tornado in *The Wizard of Oz*. Usually there's just one street with old wooden buildings that look like cowboys should be inside, except it's mostly these farmer guys buying hardware and tractors and stuff. Guys who look like they don't mind getting dirty and sweaty — in fact, they prefer it. Guys who, when they get a load of the Prairie Schooner chugging down the street, they think it's some kind of joke.

And if they think the painted-up bus is strange, a funny old dude like the Dippy Hippie, with his long hair and his Hawaiian shirt, he really makes an impression in a town full of Indiana farmers.

"Howdy doody," he says to everybody when we stop to get gas or whatever, and people look at him like he just stepped out of an alien spacecraft. Mostly they nod hello and then hurry away.

Dip, he could care less what people think. He says after thirty years as a schoolteacher he's going to play hooky whenever he feels like it.

"I'm free as a bird," he says, "but that doesn't

mean I want to fly with the rest of the flock, if you know what I mean."

I don't know what playing hooky has to do with a bunch of birds. I guess all it really means is Dip is kind of different, and he likes being that way.

Anyhow, one time we come in off the highway to get gas at this place and the bus won't start. That poor old motor keeps grinding and grinding and it coughs a little but it just won't go. "Minor malfunction," Dip says. "Nothing to it," and he gets out his tool kit and opens the hood and starts messing around under there like there's nothing else he'd rather be doing.

Frank and Joanie get out of the bus and watch Dip for a while, but you can see they think it's kind of boring, working on an old motor, and they'd rather be doing something important, like raising money for orphans or whatever.

"Even a little one-horse town like this has opportunity," Frank says. He's squinting into the sun and studying the buildings on the main street like there's something hidden there, if he can only find it.

"Forget it," Joanie says, looking around and yawning. "There's nothing here for us. Just dirt and corn and farmers."

"Then I shall plant a seed," he says. "Come along, children. Make yourselves useful."

The way he marches off, it's hard not to follow.

Worm nudges me and whispers, "You notice

something? Mr. Wonderful isn't limping anymore."

She's right. Frank has gotten better all of a sudden. The ankle that got hurt so bad when he fought the robbers must have healed overnight, because he's walking along like he hasn't got a care in the world.

"A mom-and-pop deal," he says. "This should be perfect."

"Don't be stupid," Joanie says, hanging back.

What he calls a mom-and-pop deal is really a small store with a bunch of dusty cans on the shelf, and a little old bald guy behind the counter watching game shows on this portable TV.

Frank, he marches right in and says, "How's it going, Pops?" Then he takes a newspaper out of the rack and tucks it under his arm and goes, "Where's the tuna fish?"

The old guy points and Frank cuts down the aisle like he's heading for the pot of gold at the end of the rainbow. Me and Worm and Joanie can't keep up with him, he's moving so fast.

We're turning the corner of the aisle when we hear this tremendous crashing noise. *Wham-bam-crash-bang-bing*, as just about every can of food in the place goes smashing to the floor.

"Helllllllp," Frank groans out. "Helllllllp!"

When we get there, he's buried under all these cans and loaves of bread and stuff. You can tell right away he's been hurt bad, from the way his eyes are rolling back and his mouth is hanging open like he can't get enough air.

"Slipped on something," he groans. "Oh God, I think I busted my ankle."

The old guy from behind the counter is all flustered and apologizing and saying how he'll have to call an ambulance, the nearest hospital is fifty miles away.

But Frank groans some more and says a hospital won't be necessary.

"Maybe it ain't really broke," he says. "Probably I just sprained it bad. I'll be fine."

The old guy is fussing over him and saying how sorry he is, and how maybe Frank should at least see a doctor and get the ankle checked out.

"I'll be okay, once I get my breath back," Frank says, but when he tries to walk he almost falls down, it hurts so much. Joanie has to hold up one side of him while I grab the other. "Haven't got time for broken ankles," he says. "We have to be in California in three days, isn't that right, kids?"

He's talking to me and the Worm like we're his kids, but I don't know what to say, so I just nod. The store guy looks pretty worried and you can tell he's a nice enough dude, even if he is an old geezer.

Joanie, she's busy whispering to Frank, but loud enough so you can hear her. "How can we buy groceries if we have to pay for fixing your ankle?" she says.

Frank shushes her. He's acting brave and heroic, like he doesn't want the old geezer to know how poor he is, or how he and Joanie got robbed of every earthly possession. "We'll make it somehow," he whispers real loud. "It's only three days to California. We'll eat when we get there."

The old guy hears that and gets a funny look on his face, like he's thinking hard. I'm worried maybe he's going to call the cops, but instead he fills a couple of bags with groceries. Not just cheap stuff, either, but lots of sliced meats and cheese from the cooler, and cans of tuna, and candy bars for me and Worm.

"This'll get you where you're going," he says, shoving the bags into my arms. "I hope your father has better luck in California. It can't be easy for him, not having enough money to buy food. A man'll do just about anything to put food on the table for his wife and kids, I reckon."

I'm about to tell the old guy that Frank isn't my father and we're not his children, and nobody is hungry, but he feels so good about giving us the groceries I decide to keep my trap shut.

Out on the street Frank waits until we're clear of the store, then he hands me and Worm a chocolate bar. "Good job," he says. "You've got possibilities, both of you."

Worm won't take the candy, but I figure a little chocolate won't hurt me.

You can tell Joanie isn't too impressed with

Frank. "That was just plain stupid," she tells him. "You took a risk and for what? A few slices of bologna?"

But Frank is strutting along like he's the king of the world — that ankle healed really quick this time. When he hears Joanie complaining he just grins and shakes his head. "You're missing the point, sweet buns."

"Yeah? What point is that?"

"There's a sucker born every minute. Right, Max?"

Frank has this look, like he thinks I'm in on the joke. But really I'm thinking he's right.

There *is* a sucker born every minute, and I'm one of them.

14.
The Python in the Toilet Bowl

Good old Dip has got the Prairie Schooner running real smooth by the time we get back. "Dirt in the carburetor," he says. "All those dusty roads. I see you folks have been shopping."

He's eyeballing the paper sacks and you can tell he's thinking this: If Frank got robbed of everything he owned, where'd he get the money to buy groceries?

I could explain the whole deal, but instead I chicken out and keep my mouth shut.

Worm won't say anything either, except to me. "I've read about guys like him," she whispers to me. "They lie so much they don't know what the truth is."

Frank, he must have ears like a cat, because he picks up on it. "The truth is overrated," he tells her, acting like it's a big joke we're all sharing.

"What I do is improve upon reality, and people prefer it. They really do."

After that, Dip says we should hurry up and get back on the road because you never know what might be catching up.

When we're sailing free and clear down that highway again, I start to feel better. Like what we did in the store never really happened. Like it's fading somehow, the farther away we get.

The more we stay on the Prairie Schooner the more I like it. I don't tell Worm, but inside I'm almost hoping we never get to Montana. As long as we're on the bus we're safe, and the rest of the world kind of goes away and doesn't matter as much.

Dip, he's feeling good, too, and he pops in a cassette and plays this golden oldie song about being on the road again. He punches up the volume and starts singing along like he doesn't care how bad he sounds, it's how loud that counts.

"On the road again, de doot de do, nah nah nah nah," he goes, making these electric guitar noises somewhere deep in his nose.

Joanie picks up on it right away, tapping her feet and snapping her fingers. Before you know it, she's standing up in the aisle, dancing to the music and going, "Come on! Come on!" to me and Worm.

She wants us to dance.

No way, I'd rather eat cement. You ever seen

those dancing hippos on the Disney Channel? That's me. But Joanie finally gets Worm out of her seat and makes her move to the beat, and you can tell Worm doesn't mind too much, even if she won't admit it.

"On the road again, de doot de do, nah nah nah nah!" sings Dip.

Okay, I like the song, too, even if it was old before I was born, and it's pretty hard not to sing along, and clap your hands on the beat like Joanie shows us.

Whenever we come to a good part, Dip lets loose a blast of that big old horn, *wooonnnnnnkkkkk!* and the birds fly up from the cornfields right on cue.

Frank is the only one who doesn't care about the on-the-road music. He's stretched out, taking up all of one couch, and he's got his newspaper tented over his face like he wishes we'd all shut up and let him sleep.

The weird thing is, even when he's napping he looks like he's ready to sign autographs. Like he's the star of his own personal movie and the cameras follow him everywhere. And all he has to do is look you straight in the eye and you want to be in his movie, too.

After the song ends, Joanie and Worm flop down on the couch and they're both giggling so hard they can barely breathe.

When Joanie can talk again she goes, "I needed that. Thanks, girlfriend," and pats Worm on the hand. "Who taught you to dance? Let me guess. Your brother?"

Worm shakes her head.

"Maybe it was your dad," Joanie says. "A lot of girls learn to dance from their dads."

Worm shakes her head again. Joanie doesn't seem to notice she's stopped smiling. "Had to be your mom," she says, sort of wheedling for an answer. "Did I guess right?"

Worm gets this frozen look, and her face goes so pale that her freckles look like they hurt.

"Something about your mom, huh?" Joanie says. "What happened, exactly?"

Worm curls up on the couch and covers her face with a book.

"Leave her alone," I say.

Joanie sees how Worm is hiding behind her book and she shrugs and says, "Fine. Okay. I was just making conversation. Nothing wrong with that, is there?"

I don't say anything, but my brain is thinking, *There is something wrong*, only I don't know what, exactly.

Somewhere around Illinois, Frank sits up and starts reading the newspaper. "Look here," he says. "There's a man in Topeka who found a python in his toilet. Amazing, isn't it? It says the python is native to the Amazon and somehow it got all the way to Kansas."

"Yeah," Joanie says. "Amazing."

"I bet I could make money with that snake," Frank says. "Take it on the road, sell tickets. People would pay to see a snake like that."

Joanie goes, "I'd pay more *not* to see it. Especially in the bathroom."

That shuts Frank up for a while, but he keeps rattling that newspaper just to remind us that he can see gold where everybody else just sees a python in the toilet bowl.

Late in the afternoon we cross the Mississippi River, and Dip gets real excited. "There it is!" he shouts. "Greatest waterway on planet Earth! Runs from the Minnesota lakes to the Gulf of Mexico! Passes through ten states! Over two thousand miles long! Mississippi, that means 'Big River'!"

He's talking like a geography lesson until he honks the horn and shouts, "Howdy doody, Big River!" and then he sounds like the Dippy Hippie and nobody else. "Take a look, Max. Drink it in. That's not just a river, it's liquid history. That's your country. It keeps changing paths, making its own way, just like we do."

He's so excited the Worm looks up from her book and smiles when she sees the river, which makes me think she's feeling okay again, now that Joanie has stopped asking her questions.

The Prairie Schooner sails along nice and easy until the sun goes down, and Dip says if we could go fast enough, the sun would never set because we'd chase it all the way around the world. Just thinking about that turns my brain to mush, because I know he's right and I still can't figure it out.

"Tonight we'll splurge on a real campsite," Dip announces. "If I don't get a hot shower soon, they'll put me out with the garbage."

That's how we come to stay at this KOA campground somewhere in Iowa, where they have all these Indian names but not too many Indians, not that I can see. Dip says they mostly live on reservations, but we don't have one, so we'll have to settle for the normal campground. I can tell he's pulling my leg, but I don't let on — why spoil his fun?

When the bus is parked in the right spot, Frank tucks his newspaper under his arm and says to Joanie, "I need a word with you, sweet buns."

He's acting mysterious, and he takes Joanie outside so they can talk private. I can see them under the streetlight and he's slapping his hand on the newspaper and she's listening and nodding, and I figure he's got some new scheme to get something for nothing.

Which he does, only I don't know what he has in mind, or how it's going to change everything for me and Worm and wreck our happy life in the Prairie Schooner.

If I *had* known, I'd have flushed that python right down the toilet, you can bet the ranch on that.

15.
Dip Makes a Promise

That night we're sitting around under the stars with our stomachs full. Worm has put away her book for once, and she's sitting there with her chin on her knees, staring at the little campfire Dip built. Every now and then she glances over at me like she wants to say something important, but she never does. I figure whatever it is can wait.

Frank and Joanie have wandered off somewhere, and it's just the three of us, and I'm thinking how much I want this to go on forever. Sailing that old Prairie Schooner across America, and camping by the side of the road every night, and eating hamburgers cooked over an open fire, and feeling like we're in a place of our own. I'm thinking how my buddy Kevin would have loved this adventure, and I wish he was here, and Grim and Gram, too, but even that doesn't hurt too much, I'm feeling so good.

As long as we're on the bus, the only thing that matters is where we go tomorrow. Yesterday doesn't count, or the day before that. The only thing that matters is me and Worm are safe.

I'm thinking how lucky we are right at this moment, and how no matter what happens next, I wouldn't trade this night for anything.

Dip, he's staring up at the sky for a long time and then he goes, "Guess what I see up there?"

Worm won't guess, but you can tell she's listening.

"I see a girl about your age," he says to her. "See that glow from the Milky Way? That's her hair. Those other stars are her sword and shield. She's fighting a battle. A really important battle. Life and death, I'll bet."

Worm looks up at the sky to where he's pointing. "What happens to her?" she asks.

"I'm not sure, exactly," Dips says. "But in the end she wins because her heart is true. That much I know."

Me, all I see is a bunch of stars, but I don't mind. If Worm can see her dreams come true in the sky, that's good enough. And it makes me think how cool an old dude like Dip really is, to figure it out, and show her where to look.

When Worm starts nodding off, Dip says it's time to turn in. "We have a long day tomorrow," he says. "I expect we'll see Wyoming before the sun goes down. We'll check out the Bighorn Mountains, and Yellowstone, maybe go fishing on the Wind River, if we can find some bait. Sound okay with you?"

It all sounds cool to me.

Worm is sound asleep with her backpack on, and when I pick her up to carry her inside the Prairie Schooner, she's as light as a feather, like gravity doesn't count when you're not awake.

That's when Dip goes, "Oh my."

The way he says it makes the short hairs tingle on the back of my neck. Something is wrong, I can feel it all over.

"Somebody let the air out of the tires," Dip says. "Now why would they do that?"

He's crouched down in the dark, staring at how the Prairie Schooner is sitting low on her rims. I've got Worm asleep in my arms and I don't know what to do. Flat tires are no big deal to fix, but like Dip says, why would somebody do that?

I get this terrible empty feeling like they just let the air out of me, too.

Dip gets up and says, "Wait here," and he goes into the bus and turns on the lights.

I can see him in there checking things out, and then he picks up Frank's newspaper. You can tell something has got his attention. His big friendly face kind of shuts up and I don't know what he's thinking, but whatever he's reading in the paper has made him different.

Then he looks through the bus window out to where I'm standing in the dark, and suddenly I know what's in that newspaper. Dip comes out real slow, and when his feet are on the ground he looks at how the Worm is sound asleep in my arms and he goes, "You've got ten thousand dollars on your head, Max. That's the reward for information leading to your apprehension, and for the recovery of the girl." Then he stops and gives out a big sigh, and when he speaks again his voice sounds small and old. "I knew you were in trouble. I didn't know it was trouble that big or bad."

I don't know what to do or say. It's like my feet are sinking into the ground and the sky is pressing me down and the air feels thick and scratchy in my lungs.

"I read what her stepfather had to say," he says, tapping the newspaper. "You better tell me what really happened."

"I can't," I say, whispering. "Not with her right here. She can't think about it right now, even when she's asleep."

Dip stares at me a long time and then he nods to himself and says, "Well, I guess I've got to trust my instincts on this. I'm not going to turn you in, son. But somebody else might."

That's when the flashing blue lights come gliding into the campground.

"It's my fault," Dip says when he sees those lights. "I never should have let that con man on my bus."

My feet finally come loose and I turn and see the

police car coming around the curve of the camp-sites. As it passes under a streetlight, there's Joanie in the backseat and Frank in the front. He's show-ing the cop which way to go.

"I don't know what you're going to do," Dip is saying. "But you'd better do it fast."

Then he shoves some money in my shirt pocket. He pats Worm on the head and he goes, "Trust yourself, Max. I'll see you again someday. That's a promise."

The next thing I know, I'm running off into the night with a girl in my arms, away from the Prairie Schooner and the cop car and the camp-ground. I don't know where I'm running, or why exactly. All I know is this: Worm is still asleep and she's not ready to wake up yet.

My brain has stopped thinking. The only thing inside my head is *Run, boy, run.*

16.
Sometimes the Truth Is Just Plain Stupid

The thing about running at night, you can't even see your feet, let alone the ground. You can't see the holes or the rocks or the old roots grabbing at you. The only thing to do is run faster. Fast enough so that nothing sticks. Fast enough so the shadow things can't find you. Fast enough so the dark is cool in your face, and you feel like running forever.

It's a train that finally stops me.

I'm coming down this hilly area of woods and brush, dodging around low tree branches like I've got radar or something. Like I can feel things without actually seeing them. And then I'm out of the woods and into the open, picking up speed, flying downhill like I'm an airplane getting ready to take off and Worm is my only passenger and she's still asleep.

Ahead of me something big is moving and that's when I put on the brakes and hear the screechy groan of a train grinding along the tracks. Not going fast, but kind of bumping along, *kerchunk kerchunk*, like no hurry, no problem.

There's just enough light from the stars so I can see the long, dark cars moving against the sky. They're so heavy and slow and solid it looks like they'll roll on forever, as far as the track will go.

Worm wakes up and puts her hands around my neck. "I dreamed we were flying and I wasn't afraid," she says.

I figure she'll ask me about what happened and why we ran away from Dip and the Prairie Schooner, but it's like she already knows and doesn't want to talk about it right now.

"Hold on tight," I say and she hangs on with all her might.

I start jogging along beside the track, like we're in a race or something. Me against the train. Which turns out to be going faster than I thought, because I can barely keep up.

In the movies you see dudes jump on moving trains like it was nothing. Believe me, it's not that easy, especially if you've got a girl in your arms and you've only got one hand free.

First, you have to run exactly as fast as the train is going, even though you're slipping in the gravel by the tracks and scared you'll slide under the wheels. Then you've got to grab hold of something and yank yourself aboard and not fall.

By the time we finally climb onto this low-car part of the train, I'm so scared I almost wet my pants. But Worm acts like she wasn't worried, like she knew I could do it.

"You're amazing," she says, and sounds like she really means it.

Yeah, right. The Amazing Dork.

When my heart settles down I look around. There's this big piece of farm machinery chained down to the car, but plenty of room for me and Worm to stretch out. We're barely settled when the train starts to pick up speed, and then we're rolling around this long curve, out into the countryside. I can't see much except to tell it's pretty flat and wide open.

Funny thing about the stars, when you're looking straight up they seem to hold still in the sky, even if you're on a moving railroad car. Like the stars won't change, no matter what happens. A long time ago some old dinosaur, he probably looked up and saw the same stars, mostly, and I bet he had big feet and a small brain just like me.

I know I should feel terrible about getting run off the Prairie Schooner, and having to leave the Dippy Hippie behind, but instead I'm feeling good. They didn't get us and they won't be sending Worm back to the Undertaker, not so long as we're on this train. And it's like the running part is fun, as long as you don't get caught.

Pretty dumb, huh? Well, sometimes the truth is just plain stupid, and you can't help it.

Before long, the train settles into this rhythm, rattling along the tracks, *kerchunk, kerchunk, rackety-roo, kerchunk, kerchunk, rackety-roo.*

For a long time Worm doesn't say anything, but I can tell she's thinking hard, and finally she goes, "I wasn't really asleep when the cop car came."

As usual I go, "Huh?"

"I just pretended," she says. "Because I knew Max the Mighty would come to the rescue."

Suddenly my ears feel hot and my throat is thick and part of me is mad, but I don't know why. "Cut it out," I say. "There's no such thing."

But Worm won't stop. "I heard stories about you," she says, insisting. "Kids talking. Grown-ups, too."

It makes me feel weird to think that people talk about me when I'm not around, and I bet most of it is lies.

"They said your father killed your mom, is that part true?"

I go, "Yeah," and then I'm not going to say anything else because I hate talking about it. But I'm looking at Worm and seeing how the stars make her face glow, and it's like a knot unties inside me and all of a sudden I want to tell her everything.

"It happened when I was a little kid," I say. "My dad got in a fight with my mom and he grabbed her around the neck and he wouldn't let go even though I tried to stop him. Then afterward he put me to bed and told me it was all a bad dream, but

I busted out a window and shouted for the police, and that's how he got sent to prison."

Worm doesn't say anything. She's waiting for me to finish.

"For a long time I never wanted to think about it, until Kevin and me got to be Freak the Mighty. Then he showed me how remembering can be a great invention of the mind. He said you can't forget the bad stuff because it's part of who you are."

"He was a really cool guy, huh?"

"The coolest," I say. "He even saved my life once."

"Yeah? What happened?" Worm wants to know.

"Killer Kane — that's what they call my father — they let him out of prison. Which really flipped me out. And then one night he broke into my bedroom and kidnapped me."

"How come you didn't fight him?"

I shrug. "It was like I was paralyzed or something. I just couldn't."

Worm nods and I'm pretty sure she's thinking about the Undertaker, and how he makes her feel the same way, like she can't do anything to stop him.

"Anyhow, Kevin found out where Killer Kane took me, and he figured a way to get me out of there. He filled this squirt gun with soap and vinegar and curry powder and stuff and sprayed it at my old man and we got away."

"Pretty smart," Worm says.

"Yeah. I lost it when Kevin died. It was like the whole world died, you know? Then I started thinking about all the cool things we did and I wrote some of the stuff down. And then I wasn't angry anymore, just sad. I still think about him all the time."

Worm sees how bad I'm feeling and she takes hold of my hand and gives it a squeeze and then lets go. After a while she says, "You think when you die you really go to heaven?"

"I hope so."

"Yeah," she says. "Me, too."

17.
The Horrible Howl

The *rackety-roo* of the train makes my eyelids heavy, and even though I'm supposed to stay awake and keep watch over the Worm, I fall asleep almost as soon as she does.

When I wake up again, the stars are gone and there's this orange blob on the horizon where the sun is coming up. It looks kind of hot and melted and really old somehow, like I'm looking back in time.

Worm is sleeping on my rolled-up jacket. She's holding her book tight against her chest like she always does. Probably most girls her age would throw a fit if they went to bed without a pillow, but Worm never complains about anything. When you think about what happened to her in the last few days, that's pretty amazing, and it makes me feel even better about being a notorious criminal with a ten-thousand-dollar reward on my head.

They say you can go blind if you stare at the sun too long, but I can't help it. It's like there's this message written in the sunrise and I can't quite make it out. Finally I quit looking and close my eyes, but I can still see the bright orange spot kind of burning a hole in my brain. And my brain, which is pretty irritated with me, goes, *This isn't a cool adventure, you moron! You messed up big time. The whole world thinks you're a monster for kidnapping an eleven-year-old girl. They'll hunt you down like a rabid dog. The smart thing would be to split. Let Worm find her real father on her own. Just leave her and run for your life. Keep on running until they forget all about the son of Killer Kane. Until you forget about yourself.*

I tell my brain to shut up, but it won't listen.

Leave the kid, it says. *She'll be better off without you. Somebody else can take care of her. Somebody smarter and stronger than you are. You're not a hero. Max the Mighty doesn't exist.*

"I know that!" I shout out loud, and that wakes up Worm.

She yawns and looks around and gives me a big smile. Right off she says, "You know what? I bet this train goes forever. I bet it goes to the end of the world."

All I can think to say is, "I dunno. I guess so."

Which is a flat-out lie. Even a total bonehead like me knows the world is round and you can't get to the end. You just keep going around and around and you never get there.

When the sun gets a little ways higher, the train starts to slow down and the clackety-clackety noise changes. We start passing big buildings and you can tell we're getting close to a city. I'm thinking maybe there'll be a train station and I'll be able to buy us something to eat. A hot dog or a hamburger or a candy bar — anything. Because all of a sudden I'm really, really hungry.

But when the train finally stops, there isn't any train station or any food. We're in the middle of this huge junkyard. All these cars crushed up into rusty cubes of steel, and stacked five or six high in row after row.

A wicked-looking barbed-wire fence surrounds the junkyard and I'm thinking who would want to steal a squished-up car? That's when Worm says, "Good doggie. Good doggie."

I go, "Huh?" and then I see the dog.

It's a really mangy-looking animal without a collar or a tag and it looks like it's been rolling in the dirt, or worse. From the way the ribs stick out it doesn't get fed regular and when Worm puts out her hand the dog starts edging closer, keeping low like dogs do when they're afraid.

"Oh," Worm says. "Can we keep it?"

I go, "Be careful."

"I always wanted a dog," Worm explains. "But You Know Who said no."

The dog is growling deep in its throat and its eyes don't look friendly. I grab hold of Worm's jacket and pull her back — just as the dog snaps at her hand.

"Hey!" she says. "You scared him!"

But the growling dog doesn't look scared anymore. It makes a high yipping noise, and then things start to happen fast. Because the yipping was like a signal, and now three, four, five wild dogs come out of nowhere and leap into the railway car, heading right for us.

"Get back!" I yell, grabbing Worm around the waist.

I climb onto the piece of farm equipment that's chained to the railway car and the wild dogs are leaping up and snapping their fangs, lunging at my feet.

One of the dogs grabs hold of Worm's sleeve and tears at her jacket. "Ahhh!" she screams. "Get it off! Get it off!"

The sleeve rips and the dog falls but it doesn't matter because the rest of the dogs are scrambling up on one another's backs, fighting to get higher, wanting to rip us to shreds. It's like they can smell the blood inside us, and it doesn't matter that we're human, all that matters is we might be good to eat.

Worm is crying and holding tight to me, like she thinks I can save her. But there's nowhere to go. We're surrounded, and now the dogs are crawling up the other side of the farm equipment. They'll be able to jump on us from the top.

I want to yell for help but my throat is squeezed so tight all that comes out is a pathetic little squeak. Then a dog has me by the ankle and I'm trying to kick it loose but it won't let go and Worm is screaming and kicking and hanging on to me all at the same time.

I figure this is it, we're going to die, when all of a sudden this loud, horrible howl fills the air.

"Ahhhhh-oooooooooooohhhhh!"

And this scrawny little dude with a big stick leaps into the middle of the dogs, swinging the stick and howling at the top of his lungs.

"Ahhhh-ooooooooohhhh!   Ahhhh-ooooooooohhhh!" He's screaming and laughing and yelling like a total lunatic, smacking at the dogs with his stick, kicking at them with his feet.

The dogs don't know what he is and they start yelping and ducking away from his stick, and one by one they jump off the railway car and run off into the junkyard, crawling on their bellies to get under the barbed-wire fence.

The last dog makes a lunge at his stick, but the wild man raises it high and the dog turns tail and runs off.

And that's how we got saved by Hobo Joe.

18.
Keep Us Safe from You Know Who

That's what the skinny little dude calls himself, Hobo Joe. He's got long scraggly hair and scruffy old clothes that are way too big for him and when he smiles his teeth are kind of crooked. Also he's got this wispy little mustache that wiggles when he talks, and he's talking so fast I can barely sort out the words.

"Yes, sir, they call me Hobo Joe and I'm sorry about them dogs! I bet they give you a fright, and I shoulda warned you 'cause that junkyard is famous for the pack of wild dogs. That's right, I seen you two get on back there in Iowa and I says to myself, now Joe, they'll want to rest a bit, so you best wait until morning before you drop by for a visit. See, I been riding three cars up, a nice empty boxcar with a pile of hay to sleep on, it's better than the Ritz Hotel. Got me a room with a view and room service, too. Hey, I'll bet you two ain't had breakfast, am I right about that? Huh? Am I?"

"Excuse me?" I ask, because listening to some-body talk that fast makes my ears ring.

"Food," he says. "Breakfast. I got it if you want some."

Breakfast is this great big can of beans that Joe had been heating up over a Sterno can when the dogs attacked us. Now he heats it up again and pretty soon the smell of simmering beans is thick in the air.

"I know what you're thinkin'," he says. "You're thinkin' a can of beans don't make a breakfast. But that's where you're wrong, because beans is the best kind of food. 'Specially when you're hungry."

Normally I could care less about beans, but we haven't had a thing to eat since supper last night and the sight of those beans bubbling away makes my mouth water. I ask Worm if she's hungry and she nods and Joe shows her how to blow on the spoon so she won't burn her mouth.

"These beans got special vitamins," he says. "Make you grow big and strong."

He's got this old canvas bag he keeps his stuff in, and inside is a loaf of bread. Stale bread with a hard crust. But Joe says it'll soften up good in the bean juice and we tear up the bread and soak it and stuff it in our mouths until we can't eat an-other bite.

If you're hungry enough, stale bread and beans taste better than birthday cake.

While we're eating, Joe never stops talking and moving around. Like he's got batteries inside that make him keep jumping and fidgeting and twitching his fuzzy little mustache.

"Guests for breakfast," he says. "Who'd a thunk it!" and he rattles on about how lonesome it gets, living on the trains, and how he's glad of the company and how good it is to have someone to talk to because mostly he talks to himself, and how talking to yourself doesn't necessarily mean you're crazy because there has to be an exception to every rule and he, Hobo Joe, is the talking-to-himself exception.

After we spoon up the last of the beans, the boxcar gives a shudder and starts moving again.

"They been shunting off some of the freight cars," Joe explains. "That means they unhook 'em and leave 'em behind. Train'll be lighter now, and faster. By the time we clear Nebraska we'll be flyin', yessir!"

He knows so much about trains because he's been living off the land, he says, and riding the rails from one side of the country to the other and then back again. So he knows what train goes where, and why it stops at one place instead of another, and how not to get caught by the railroad police.

"Don't be thinkin' I'm homeless," he explains to

Worm. "Wherever I'm sleepin', that's my home, and I like it fine." He points at the wide open door of the boxcar, and the prairie grass rushing past like a blurry green river. "Can you beat that? Why it's better than TV!"

It sounds strange, but staring out at the countryside really is better than watching TV, because you never know what you're going to see next. Farms and barns and windmills. Tall silvery silos that look like spaceships ready to take off. Railroad bridges built from giant Erector sets. A herd of buffalo that look like cows with fur coats on. There's even some purple mountains way off in the distance, just like in the song about America.

Everything keeps moving. It never settles into one thing, it keeps moving and turning into something new. You don't need to change the channel, because it keeps changing itself and never stays the same.

After a while I feel like I'm getting hypnotized. Like I'm wide-awake but dreaming. Like the train is standing still and the world is turning under us.

Worm, she gets tired of watching the world go by and takes out a new book. This one is called *The Sword in the Stone*. I know about it because Kevin read it and told me the story back before I could read on my own.

It's about this kid who everyone thinks is a real loser until one day he accidentally pulls this sword out of a stone. And that proves he's going to grow up to be King Arthur, this excellent dude who had a posse of knights in shining armor, slaying dragons and rescuing damsels, which are what they called women in the old days.

"You know what's so cool about King Arthur and his Knights of the Round Table?" Worm says to me. "It's all about fighting for honor and protecting the innocent and never giving up even if the whole world is against you."

I go, "Yeah, that's pretty cool."

"The coolest thing is, they called it chivalry," Worm says, sounding excited. "And that's where we're going. Chivalry, Montana."

She acts like it's this big coincidence, but I'm pretty sure she knew about knights and chivalry, and that's why she picked the book in the first place, so it would remind her of where we're headed.

"You sure your dad is there?" I ask her.

For some reason that makes her mad. "You don't believe me, is that it? You want me to swear on my grave? Okay, I swear on my grave: My father is in Chivalry, Montana!"

I go, "Okay, okay. Take it easy."

Joe hears her and butts in. "Chivalry? That where you two are headed?"

Worm glares at me and then nods. "Yes," she says. "Most definitely."

"Then you come to the right place," Joe says. "This train don't go there, exactly, but I know one that does."

"And you'll show us?"

"'Course I will," he says. "But it ain't exactly right around the corner. We got a good long while before we get there, so if you guys don't mind, I'm gonna catch up on my beauty sleep."

Joe fluffs up his canvas bag like it's a pillow and stretches out his skinny legs and closes his eyes. Pretty soon you can hear him snoring and it blends into the sound of the train.

Worm taps me on the shoulder. "Sorry I got mad," she says.

I go, "That's okay."

"It's just I miss my mom," Worm says.

"Sure," I say. "That's only natural."

The Worm looks fierce. "I miss her but I hate her guts."

I go, "Huh?"

"It's her fault," Worm says. "She didn't have to marry that creepoid. Or let him hurt me. Or lie to the cops."

"She's scared of him," I say. "People do stupid things when they're scared."

"But she's my *mom*. Moms are supposed to take care of you."

I don't know what to say. Moms aren't supposed to die, either, but sometimes they do.

"Everything will be okay if I can just talk to

my dad," Worm says. "My real dad. He'll understand."

"Don't worry," I say. "We'll find him."

Then everything is quiet except for the clickety sound of the train and the wind humming by. It's so quiet I can hear my own heart beating and it seems to go *rackety-roo, rackety-roo* just like the train.

After a while Worm tugs at my arm and says, "You hear that? It sounds like giants talking under the earth."

At first I think it's just another weird thing she got out of a book, but then I start to hear it, too. A low rumble that seems to come off the mountains and roll over the plains. You can't quite make out the words. You can't tell if they're just talking or fighting or maybe the giants are singing and it sounds like earthquakes and avalanches from far, far away.

"It's like they're calling us," Worm says in a whispery soft voice. "Trying to tell us something."

I'm listening so hard my ears are hot, and finally I figure it out. The rumble noise from the train is echoing off the mountains. That's what makes it sound so hollow and deep. It's not giants talking under the earth, it's only the lonesome sound the train makes as it goes through the world.

But I don't say anything and Worm keeps listening, and she's smiling to herself, like she knows what the giants are saying, and that makes everything okay.

I can't hear the giants anymore, but there's a song coming from inside the train. *Rackety-roo, rackety-roo. Keep us safe from You Know Who.*

19.
Wide-Open Country

Joe wakes up fresh as a daisy, he says. He leans out the door of the boxcar and takes a sniff and goes, "Wyoming! I can smell Wyoming just around the bend! Better than perfume! Smells like dry dirt and tumbleweeds!"

He says he's been through this way before but he never gets tired of it. "I love this wide open country," he says. "I bet you can see a hundred miles at least. See that mountain over there, against the dark patch of sky? Seems so close you could hit it with a rock, don't it? Just you try! You could walk all day for a week and still you wouldn't be close. What it is about the West, the real West, the scale is different. The sky is higher up and wider open and that makes everything bigger. Makes a man look to himself because there's nobody else can see him! Yessir!"

So we roll on into Wyoming and Joe says the train is probably making sixty miles an hour. Just humming along, running straight into the horizon, and nothing around but a few scrubby pine trees and these far-off mountains that look like somebody painted them against the sky.

Every now and then the train stops, and Joe always knows where we are and why we stopped, and if we should change boxcars. "They got to fuel up those diesel engines," he'll say. Or, "They're pickin' up a ten-car hitch out of Casper."

Pretty much every time we stop, Joe disappears for a little while and then comes back with some kind of food. He never says exactly where he finds it, but when you're hungry and riding the rails you don't ask too many questions.

He'll heave up this big sack of oranges and go, "Nobody'll miss these little beauties. Got to get our vitamins!"

Maybe he'll bring back a box of stale crackers and a big restaurant tin of honey and give it over to Worm and say, "Nothin' wrong with these crackers a little honey won't fix!"

Thanks to our skinny friend, we never get so hungry we can't stand it. Not that the Worm eats much, but Joe bets I could win one of those flapjack-eating contests where a bunch of lumberjacks eat until they bust. "It ain't just a hollow leg with you," he says, "it's a hollow everything. Which means you're still growing! Pardon me, son, but if you get any bigger you're gonna need your own time zone!"

For some reason I don't mind it when Joe kids me about being big. Maybe because he's so small and scrawny. Maybe because he doesn't have much of anything, but he always shares it without making you feel like he's doing you a favor. And he never asks what me and Worm are doing on our own, or tries to give us a bunch of advice about what we should do and why.

Most important, any time Worm looks a little sad or unhappy, Joe is right there working to cheer her up. "Look over there," he says, getting her attention. "No, farther out. You see that thing moving up and down? Looks like a big tipped-over swing set? That's an oil pump. That's right, they're raising oil out of a deep well. They'll put a pump like that wherever they find oil. Once I seen one right in a churchyard! Talk about an answer to your prayers!"

Worm stares out at the horizon. "They look like giant birds pecking at the dirt," she says.

When Joe hears that, he doesn't make fun of her, he just nods to himself and goes, "I never thought of it that way. Giant birds, huh?"

We're heading out through the wide-open spaces for hours and hours. Pretty soon we'll cross over into Montana, Joe says, where the last of the cowboys live, and the mountains reach all the way to the moon, and that's where we change trains to Chivalry.

Joe says we're on the right track, yessir, and it feels good.

The way night happens out West, the sun kind of disappears all at once and suddenly the stars are shining and the air feels thin and cool. Worm has got herself real comfortable on this pile of hay Joe fluffed up, reading with her miner's light, and before long her chin starts to droop and then she's fast asleep. I shut off the light to save the battery and Joe brings out this old wool blanket and covers her.

Me and Joe are both shivering a little, but it feels good watching Worm sleep so calm and peaceful under that warm blanket.

"I guess you know she's pretty special," Joe says.

I don't say anything because I hate gooey talk like that, but it makes me think about how sometimes you meet someone who really messes up your life but you'd rather have a messed-up life than not know them.

Anyhow, everything will be okay if we can just find her father. And because we got lucky and bumped into Joe, now we're headed in the right direction.

I never do fall asleep. There's something wide-awake inside my head that makes me think of Grim and Gram and how much I miss them, and how rotten it was for me to run off without telling them why, or even saying good-bye. I keep thinking how much they've done for me and how I never did anything much for them, except a couple of lame presents at Christmas or whatever.

When the sun finally comes up, I'm still thinking about home, and how there's no place I'd rather be but hanging out in the down under and reading my comic books for the umpteenth time.

So I'm already feeling pretty low down and sorry for myself when Joe tells me the bad news.

"We're almost there," he says, out of the blue.

I go, "Huh?"

"You kids want to get to Chivalry, right? Well, I got you on the right train. All you gotta do is ride it to the end and you'll be there."

"But what about you?" I ask. "You're coming, too, right?"

Joe shakes his head. "I got business elsewhere," he says. "I got to keep moving, I can't stay still."

Which shows you what a doughnut brain I can be, because I'd been thinking somehow we'd stay on the train forever and just keep riding through the wide-open spaces, and Joe would always be there to tell us where we were, and what was going to happen next.

The train starts slowing down, and gets so slow you could walk beside it.

"There's apples and that tin of American cheese," Joe says, getting ready to go. "I left a big can of beans, too."

"What about your blanket?" I say, looking at where Worm is still curled up and sound asleep.

"Better keep it," he says. Before he hops down from the boxcar he says, "Here's the deal. In about a hundred miles this train dead-ends in Chivalry. Hope you find what you're looking for."

Then he slips over the side and he's gone. The last thing I hear is his voice sounding far away already.

"Yessir!" he calls out. "Don't forget them beans! They got vitamins!"

20.
Chivalry

We're alone again when Worm finally wakes up.

"I dreamed I was home in my own bed," she says. Then she stops herself, like there are parts of the dream she doesn't want to talk about.

I explain about Joe leaving, and how the last stop is supposed to be Chivalry. When I say how everything will be okay once she finds her real father, Worm stares down at her hands and won't say anything. Which really blows my mind, because she's supposed to be happy and excited, right?

Worm has never been a big talker, but the closer we get to where we're going, the less she says. Like she's got this big secret and not talking is the only way to keep it all to herself.

Meanwhile the train takes a long time rolling up toward the end of the line. Moving along in fits and starts. Every time we stop I lean out real careful and take a look around and sometimes I spot these railroad guys waving their arms and shouting out orders. If they suspect anybody is sneaking a ride on their train, it's like they don't care, or they don't want to know.

The mountains are right up close around here. You can see where they start and how they jut up so fast and steep it makes you dizzy looking all the way to the top. The mountains seem like they're made of yellow dirt and yellow rock and a few scrawny-looking bushes here and there, like nothing can grow on a place that steep without falling off.

One time the train stops inside a tunnel and it's so dark it might as well be midnight. Worm switches on her light, but she isn't reading, she's using it to look at me. "I had this weird idea that we all disappear when the lights go out," she says. "Not just you, but me, too."

I go, "That's weird all right."

"Like they say, maybe there's no such thing as a noise if there's no one to hear it."

"Who says that?" I ask.

"Just 'they,' " she says. "I don't know who."

"Well, 'they' sound pretty stupid to me," I say. Which ends the conversation right there. Worm switches off the light and I figure she's hoping I really *have* disappeared.

I'm thinking: What am I going to do with a girl

who doesn't know what's real and what's just in her head? I'm thinking: Here we are in the dark, stuck inside a mountain in a place I've never been and we're about a million miles from home and we don't have the Dippy Hippie to help us, or Hobo Joe, or anybody at all, and I haven't got a clue about what to do.

That's when my brain says, *I told you so, you moron*, and my brain is right, because it's been telling me all along that running away was a big mistake.

After a while, Worm's voice comes out of the dark. "Are you still there?"

I go, "Yeah."

"Good," she says, and then she shuts up again.

Suddenly the train goes *bump-bump* and starts moving again, and we slowly come out from under the mountain and back into daytime.

At first the light makes me squint so hard I can't really see anything. But pretty soon I can make out these shiny roofs and a bunch of chimneys and stuff.

We're looking down on this town full of junky old wooden buildings stuck right up against the bottom of the mountains. There's only one road and it's just plain dirt, no paving. The roofs are shiny because they're made of tin, but when you look closer you can see streaks of rust and dark spots that must be holes. There's a couple of old trucks, but the hoods are up and they look broke down forever.

I keep expecting to see people going in and out of the buildings, or maybe kicking the tires on those old trucks, but the only thing moving is a broken door slapping in the breeze. It looks like everybody just walked away from Chivalry and never came back.

I always wondered what a ghost town was. Now I know.

21.
What the Owl Knows

Now that Chivalry turns out to be this falling-down old place where nobody normal would ever live, I'm starting to think maybe Worm's father is going to turn out to be even weirder than she is. He's probably some old hermit with a long white beard, or one of those guys who walk around in camouflage gear talking to themselves about what happened in the war.

Okay, so maybe finding Worm's real dad won't solve everything. But at least I won't be the only one looking out for her. And even if my brain doesn't think so, I'm hoping he can help clear it up with the police, and make it so everybody doesn't think I'm a kidnapper, or worse.

"You sure this is the right place?" I ask as the train rolls through the little town.

Worm nods. She hasn't said a word since we

came out of the tunnel, and she's not reading her book, either. Her eyes have this look that's either scared or excited, maybe both.

The old train station is built right up against the side of the mountain. It's all boarded up with plywood covering the doors and windows. Which doesn't do much good because part of the roof has caved in.

Near the train station I notice a faded sign that says,

CHIVALRY MINING CORPORATION
"We're Digging for the Future!"

I doubt this is the future they had in mind, with everybody gone and the whole town falling down. From the look of everything, they must have run out of stuff to mine, and that's why nobody is around.

All of a sudden the train motors stop and you can feel the way everything goes dead quiet.

"We better get out of here," I say. Because sooner or later those railroad guys are going to check the boxcars and never mind what my stupid brain says, I'm not ready to get caught yet.

Worm helps me load up with apples and cheese and the other food Joe left behind.

"You know where your father lives?" I ask.

Worm shakes her head no.

"But you're sure he's here?" I ask.

"I'm sure," she says, but her voice sounds so small it's like she swallowed something the wrong way.

We slip away from the boxcar without being seen and skid down this gravel embankment until we're out of sight of the train. Worm stays close to me while I check out the old buildings, looking for a good place to hide until we can find her real father, or until he finds us.

I'm kind of spooked, because it feels like something is watching us from inside the ratty old buildings, like the empty windows are really eyes. The sound of a broken door slamming in the wind is driving me nuts.

"Come on," I say, and we head straight for the banging door. It's on the back side of this boarded-up building that has gray clapboards peeling off and a saggy old front porch that faces the dirt street.

The first step through that busted door almost breaks my leg.

Wham! My foot goes through the floorboards and I fall sideways. The air gets whumped out of me so bad I can't say anything, I just have to lie there and wheeze for a while.

Worm asks me four or five times if I'm okay, which I am once my breath comes back.

The place is pretty dim except where beams of sunlight come through the boarded-up windows and the holes in the roof. The inside is basically one room with a few broken chairs and a tipped-over table with three legs. There's a big wooden counter along one wall that looks kind of familiar. Then it comes to me.

"I bet this used to be an Old West saloon," I tell Worm. "Only it was probably miners instead of cowboys."

The only thing is, it looks a whole lot crummier than the neat old saloons you see in the movies, where Maverick and his buddies are sitting around playing cards and acting cool. You couldn't act cool in this place no matter what you did.

"How will your dad know you're here?" I ask.

"He'll know," she says. Like that's final, end of discussion.

I'm feeling my way along in case there's any more soft spots in the floor. The more I look, the more junk I see. Empty bottles, cracked mugs, a box of candles, a broken mirror in a fancy frame, an old tin of wooden matches.

Worm has her head cocked to one side, listening hard. "Can you hear them?" she whispers.

"Hear who?" I ask.

"All the people who went away. It sounds like they're whispering."

"That's only the wind," I say.

"I hear *something*," she insists.

I go, "It's just your imagination."

That makes her frown at me, but she does shut up about the whispering ghosts.

115

Probably this whole town has been checked out, and everything valuable got swiped. But you never know what might get missed, so I'm poking around behind the old wooden bar when suddenly I feel somebody watching me.

I turn around real careful and slow.

Eyes!

Right in front of me, close enough to touch, these big yellow eyes are looking at me. Real eyes. Eyes that are alive inside. The eyes blink and I can't breathe or talk or scream out how scared I am.

Below the staring eyes is this strange, sharp-curved nose. Then I realize it isn't a nose, exactly. It's a beak.

Owl. I'm staring at an owl, a great big brown-and-white owl, and he's looking at me like he could care less. It comes to me so sudden that I fall back on my heels and sort of tip over backward, *thump!*

The noise startles the owl from his perch under the bar and he opens his beak and goes, "*Hooooooooo!*" He unfolds these huge wings and launches himself up into the air and takes off.

"*Hooooooo!*" he goes. "*Hooooooooo! Hooooooooooo!*"

The big owl flaps around the inside of the ratty old saloon and his wings make a whispery sound like "*Wissshhhhh! Wisssssshhhhh!*"

The Worm never screams, not once. She just stands there and watches, her eyes almost as big around as the owl's.

After I get over being scared to death, the big old owl starts to look sort of beautiful. It's amazing how it swoops so calm and cool around the room, wings never quite touching the walls. It doesn't look like a normal bird, it looks more human because both eyes are in front. It makes you understand why they say owls are wise. Man, this bird looks like it knows everything. How old the earth is, why the sky is blue, where you hid your favorite comic book, everything.

The owl goes, "*Hooooooooooooooooooooooo!*" and swoops up into the wrecked part of the roof and then he's gone.

"Wow," I say, and let out the breath I've been holding.

I look over to see Worm staring up at where the owl found a way out to the sky. She's got this secret look on her face like somehow she knows what the owl knows.

22.
Magic Believes in Me

Nothing tastes better than apples and good old American cheese when your mouth is dry and your stomach is growling. After the owl takes off, me and Worm decide it's time for lunch. I'm expecting she'll want to go look for her dad first thing, but she doesn't seem to be in any hurry to find him now that we're here.

Mostly she just watches me eat. Worm doesn't seem to have much appetite.

"Apple a day keeps the bad guys away," I say, trying to joke her into eating.

She just scowls at me and gnaws her apple a little.

"Beans?" I ask. "We could heat 'em up over a candle."

She shakes her head.

After a while, when my stomach isn't so empty

anymore, I lean back and go, "How come your dad lives in an old ghost town?"

Worm stares at her hands. "Because he does," she says. "I don't want to talk about him right now, okay?"

"Okay," I say.

I'm not exactly surprised when Worm pulls a book out of her backpack. When she doesn't want to talk about something, she always goes right for her books.

"What are you reading now?" I ask.

She holds the book up. "*The Hobbit*," she says. "I've read it before."

"Me, too," I say.

Worm gets this look like she can't believe the big goon can actually read a book, and for some reason that really burns me. "What," I say. "You think you're the only one who ever read a book?"

She shrugs. "I didn't say that."

"No, but that's what you're thinking, right? Because I'm this big goofy-looking guy who doesn't talk that much, I must be dumb."

She goes, "I never said that."

"No, but that's what you're thinking," I say. Then I shut up quick, because Worm looks like she's going to cry. Which proves that I really am a big doughnut brain, even if I do know how to read.

She sits there with her chin on her knees and her eyes closed, not moving at all. I'm starting to wonder if she's fallen asleep when she goes, "You know what? The first time I read *The Hobbit* I wanted to *be* Bilbo Baggins, you know? And live in a hobbit hole underground and have friends like Gandalf the wizard, and go on adventures to the Lonely Mountain, and fight Smaug the evil dragon."

"Really?" I say. "That's what I thought, too."

After that something breaks loose and she can't stop talking about all these books she's read, and how much it means to her, and how she's probably a book addict but she doesn't care, and how she doesn't even mind everybody calling her Worm because it's an honor to be a bookworm even if nobody understands.

"You know what's really weird?" she says. "All those kids who make fun of me and act like such jerks, they really feel sorry for me, right? But *I'm* the one who feels sorry for *them*. They're the ones who don't know about how Charlotte saved Wilbur. Or why Old Yeller had to die. Or how the boy saved the dog named Shiloh."

Worm is so excited she's punching her fist in the air and her eyes are blazing and her hair is so red and wild it looks like her head is on fire. I'm ready to applaud but I figure she'd probably take it wrong and punch me out. It's like there's a whole other person living inside her that only comes out when she talks about books, and that person is so brave that nothing could scare her.

———

It must have been really miserable being a caveman, before fire got invented. I know because when night comes and it starts to get cold, the first thing we try to do is make a fire and get warm. There's this little potbellied stove in the saloon and plenty of busted-up chairs and old newspapers and stuff, so I figure it won't be hard.

Wrong.

The wooden matches are so old they keep falling apart. I'm scratching the side of the box and the heads keep snapping off or going soft or whatever and before you know it we're down to one match.

One measly crummy match.

That's when I notice Worm is sitting there grinning in the dark. "We'll have to use magic," she says.

"There's no such thing as magic, except in books."

Worm shakes her head. "Not true," she says. "Book magic escapes into the real world."

She sounds so convinced I decide not to argue. If you think about the raw deal Worm has been getting, you can't blame her for wanting to believe in magic and wizards and hobbits. If she can fill her head with stuff like that, she won't have to think about the bad things that have already happened, and what might happen next if we don't find her real father.

"I'll show you," she says, and holds out her hand.

I shrug and give her the last match.

"Watch and believe," she says.

Then she takes all of her books out of her backpack and makes a pile on the floor. She opens each book and waves the match over it and goes, "Humnahooah, humnahooah, give us fire, give us light, keep us warm on this cold night!"

After she's waved the last matchstick over each and every book, she hands it back to me.

"That's it?" I ask. "That's the magic?"

She nods. "No problem. Guaranteed to light."

I look at the measly match and I'm thinking, Go ahead, what have you got to lose? But then my brain says, *Don't be a dodo, you big moron. If the match doesn't light, that will mean books aren't magic, and where does that leave the Worm?*

Now I wish I'd never tried to light a stupid fire. But it's getting colder by the minute and all we've got is that one old blanket Joe left us, so what choice do I have?

When I scratch the last match on the side of the box, *poof!* a blue flame pops up and I'm so surprised I almost forget to put it in the stove and light the fire.

"It's like clapping for Tinkerbell," Worm explains when we're warming our hands in front of the stove. "You don't dare not believe it."

The real truth is, I still don't believe in magic. But I'm starting to wonder if maybe magic believes in me.

23.
The Secret of Chivalry

Just when I'm falling asleep, the owl comes back.
He flies in through the hole in the roof as quiet as
a whisper. His wings seem to fill up the night.
Normally I'd be scared, a big thing like that
swooping around in the dark, but there's a lot of
other stuff crowding my brain lately.

So I lay there staring at the glow from the wood-
stove, trying as hard as I can not to think about the
trouble we're in. Like running away from the
scene of a crime and lying about who we are and
believing a phony like Frank and escaping from
the police. Stupid stuff like that.

My brain is thinking, *You better start acting smart,*
you big jerk, and it won't let me sleep. It makes me
count the stupid things I've done instead of counting sheep or whatever. I'm counting every stupid
thing I ever said or did in school that made

everybody laugh at me, and all the words I didn't understand back then, and all the books I never read, and all the cool things I wish I'd said but didn't, and all the time I wasted being mad at the world when I was really mad at me, and that day my pants fell down in gym class, and the time Kevin dared me to eat a tadpole for scientific purposes, and I did and got sick.

All of it starts whirring around inside my brain, the really bad stupid stuff and the just plain stupid stuff and the who cares stupid stuff, until it feels like there's an eggbeater inside my head turning my brain into scrambled eggs. Which makes me feel even *more* stupid.

Then my brain has an idea. *Leave the girl here and turn yourself in*, it tells me. *You know that's the smart thing to do.*

You mean leave Worm on her own? I ask my brain.

She's the one who wanted to run away. She's the one who wanted to find her real father. So let her. If you stay with her, you're the one who will get the blame.

Just go? I ask my brain. Sneak away while she's sound asleep?

Do the smart thing.

Sorry, I tell my brain. I can't leave Worm, not now. Not here. Not when we've come this far. Her dad is going to fix everything.

You're hopeless, my brain says. But finally it lets me fall asleep, and in my dream we're back on the Prairie Schooner with good old Dip, and Joe is there, too, and we're all going home and everything is going to be okay, just like on TV.

In the morning Worm says it's time to find her real dad.

"He's waiting for me," she says. "Out there."

She's staring at her hands again, like she doesn't want me to see what she's hiding in her eyes.

I go, "You know where he is?"

Worm nods.

"I don't get it," I say. "If you know where he is, why didn't we go there right away?"

Worm shrugs. "I wasn't ready."

She's not going to tell me what's really going on, or why she's being so mysterious.

Outside the old saloon, Worm takes a deep breath, squints into the sunlight, and starts marching up the street, like she knows exactly where she wants to go.

I'm tagging along, tripping over my big feet, and saying stuff like, "So what's the deal? Where are we going?"

Worm doesn't say anything, she just balls her hands into fists and keeps on marching.

We pass all of these falling-down old buildings, places that once upon a time were a general store or a barbershop or whatever, and we're heading up the slope toward the mountain that looms over the whole town.

"The railway station," I say. "He's at the railway station? Why didn't you say so?"

The old railway station is the biggest building around, with tons of fancy trim and a steep roof with a big chunk missing. It looks kind of like a gingerbread house except all the icing has melted off. You can tell the people who used to live here must have sunk everything into this one building, to make an impression when visitors came to Chivalry, and maybe to kind of inspire the rest of the town. It didn't catch on, that's for sure, and now the train only comes here because it's a good place to turn around, which is pretty pathetic, if you think about it.

Anyhow, when we get to the railway station I'm expecting some weird old guy to pop out of the woodwork and go, "Hey, kids! I'm Rachel's dad!" or whatever, and we'll have to go from there. But when we get there, nothing happens. There's nobody waiting for us.

Worm stares hard at the building. "Inside," she says.

"It's boarded up," I point out. "We can't get inside."

But Worm won't take no for an answer. It's pretty clear she's going to find a way into the railway station or die trying, so we go around back. Only there isn't any back to the building because it's built right up against the side of the mountain. And everything is boarded up and nailed shut with these big spikes you couldn't pull out with a crowbar even if you had one, which I don't.

Finally Worm finds a hole in the wall. "Here goes nothing," she says.

"Wait up!" I say. "Hang on!"

But she's already inside.

It turns out the hole is just barely big enough for a doofus like me to wriggle through if I hold my breath. I end up facedown on the floor with dust in my eyes and that makes it hard to see. But even without seeing you can feel how big it is inside the railway station, much bigger than it looks on the outside.

When my eyes start to clear up I can make out the rows of old benches where people must have waited for the train, and the ticket windows. Everything else seems to blend into the shadows. It can be anything you want it to be, or nothing at all.

But the inside of the station isn't all dark places. There's this one beam of sunshine coming down through the hole in the roof and the Worm is standing right inside the light.

"Dad!" she calls out. "It's me, Rachel! Are you there?"

And then she says it again and again, *there-there-there-there*. Except her mouth isn't moving. It's an echo coming back from someplace deep inside the earth.

Which is impossible but true.

My eyes have gotten used to the dim and dusty light and I can see it now.

A tunnel.

The echo is coming from a mining tunnel that goes straight back into the mountain. A tunnel so big and dark it looks like it wants to swallow up all the light in the world, and us, too.

Something about that old mining tunnel scares me like nothing ever scared me before. Somehow I know there's evil and misery inside, just waiting until somebody comes along and lets it out.

"Dad!" Worm shouts, and it comes back *Dad-Dad-Dad-Dad*.

I may be big and dumb, and a lot of times I won't listen to my brain, but it doesn't take me long to figure out that if her real father is down in this old mine, he probably isn't coming out.

When I get to Worm, she's shining her miner's light on a bronze plaque near the entrance to the mine, where the railroad tracks curve into the darkness and disappear.

On the plaque it says:

> BURIED IN THIS SHAFT
> ARE THE REMAINS
> OF SIXTY-SEVEN MEN
> WHOSE LIVES WERE LOST
> IN THE GREAT CHIVALRY
> MINE DISASTER.
> MAY GOD HAVE MERCY
> ON THEIR SOULS,
> AND ON THOSE
> THEY LEFT BEHIND.

Worm goes, "Daddy, I miss you so much. Please tell me what to do. Please?"

The echo comes back *ease-ease-ease*.

My brain tells me I should have known it all along. The reason Worm's real father has never been there to help her is because he's dead. We've come all this way just so she can visit his grave, and we can't even do that because he doesn't have a grave of his own, not like in a real cemetery.

Worm finally notices me and takes a tight grip on my hand. "I was so little when it happened I can barely remember him," she says. "All I remember is he had this miner's helmet with a light, and I wanted one, too."

There's nothing I can think to say except, "He must have been a pretty cool dad, giving his kid her own miner's helmet."

Worm squeezes my hand so hard it hurts, and it makes me think she's a lot stronger than she looks.

"Do you think he knows about my mom?" she asks. "And You Know Who?"

I never get to answer that one because a new sound comes into the old railway station and starts echoing back out of the tunnel.

It's a siren. A cop car siren.

24.
Officer Friendly

I find a crack to look out through the boarded-up windows. The siren has stopped whooping, but there it is, a white cop car kicking up dust as it comes down the main street, heading for the railway station. The cop car has a big star on the side, and SHERIFF spelled out in gold.

Worm is looking out through the same crack and she's not making a sound. She doesn't act scared, exactly. It's like she's got a switch inside and she just turns herself off somehow.

The sheriff car pulls up to the front of the station. The sun glints off the windshield so you can't see inside, but the driver's door opens right away and this short, stocky dude gets out, wearing a white cowboy hat and a gold star on his shirt pocket.

He cups his hands to his mouth and calls out, "Anybody home?"

When nothing happens, he looks around, squinting at the broken-down town. He snugs down his hat, hitches up his belt, and spits in the dirt, which I must admit he does in a pretty cool way.

Then he kind of shrugs to himself and walks back to his cop car and opens the door like he's going to get inside and drive away.

But he doesn't drive off, not yet. He comes back out of the cruiser with this shiny metal thing in his hand. At first I think it's a gun, but then he holds it up to his mouth and clicks it on.

Megaphone.

"Howdy, folks. This is Sheriff Goodman. I'm the law here in this county. If there's anybody around, please come out and say hello. Nobody gets arrested, nothing like that. Just want to make sure you're okay."

The last word echoes up from the tunnel behind us, *kay-kay-kay*, and there's nothing I'd like better than to give myself up to Officer Friendly here. Let him figure out what to do about Worm. A dude who can spit so cool can probably figure out most anything, right?

Wrong. Because my brain knows he's just acting friendly so he can get us to surrender, and then he'll lock me in jail and throw away the key and send Worm back to her rotten stepfather because in real life stuff never has a happy ending like it does on TV. I learned that a long time ago and my brain won't let me forget it.

You can tell Sheriff Goodman is listening hard,

so me and Worm don't make a peep, we hardly breathe. When he doesn't hear anything he switches on the megaphone again and goes, *"Maybe I got it wrong and there's nobody here, but if there is, please remember one thing. The old mining tunnels are very dangerous. Repeat, stay out of the tunnels."* He starts to lower the megaphone and then remembers to say, *"Have a nice day,"* before he turns it off for good.

The sheriff looks like he's about ready to give up when suddenly the passenger door swings open. At first I can't see who's there, all I can do is hear one boot hit the dirt, then the other. And then he's unfolding himself from inside the cop car and standing tall and thin and dark as a shadow.

The Undertaker, come to get us.

25.
Things That'll Turn Your Bones into Jelly

Beside me Worm makes a small whimpering sound.

"I'm not here," she whispers to herself. "I'm somewhere else. I'm somewhere else." Except she doesn't sound like she believes it.

I've got my face against the crack in the window boards, trying to keep an eye on things. Sheriff Goodman is still there, but I can't see Worm's stepfather, like he's moved out of range.

Suddenly the board gets yanked off the window and a blast of daylight hits me right in the face.

The Undertaker is on the other side of the window, looking in at both of us. He lifts up his hand and points at me and shouts, "There he is! The monster who kidnapped my daughter!"

His raggedy lightning voice goes through me like a hot bullet and for a moment my heart just stops. I can't move.

Sheriff Goodman goes, "You'd better come out of there. I'll bet you're pretty hungry, huh? We'll get us some food and then we'll talk."

Worm bolts. Running away as fast as she can.

Before my brain knows what's going on, my feet are following her, running into the darkness, into that old mining tunnel, into the place of the dead.

The sheriff is yelling, begging us not to go into the mine, but he's so far away he sounds like he's shouting from another planet. I'm barreling along like an out-of-control locomotive, heading for the tunnel. Racing across the floor of the old train station with the terrible darkness getting closer and closer, that's when my brain tries to put on the brakes.

Don't do it! my brain screams. *If you go down into that mine, you'll never come out alive!*

Shut up, I say to my brain, and keep on going.

But my brain won't shut up. *There are terrible things down there*, it says, *things you can't think about or you'll die. Things that'll turn your bones into jelly. Things that'll eat you up and spit you out. Things that'll make you wish you'd never been born.*

But it's too late to stop, no matter what my brain says. I'm already inside the entrance to the mine, trying to catch Worm before the shadows swallow her up. The air feels different, and the darkness feels different, and I'm running so fast there's no turning back.

I can't stop. It's like gravity is sucking me down into the mining tunnel, under the mountain, into the earth.

"Wait! *Wait-wait-wait*. . . ."

Sheriff Goodman's voice turns into an echo. The words chase us underground. I'm still running as hard as I can, down into the darkness, and the last thing I hear is him shouting, "Be careful-*ful-ful-ful*. . . ."

Too late for that. I'm way past being careful.

And that's the last thing in my head before something comes out of the dark and *whams!* me so hard my bones turn to jelly, just like my brain promised.

Some people see stars when they get knocked out. Me, I see mosquitoes. Shiny mosquitoes buzzing around my head.

They're still buzzing when Worm wakes me up. She doesn't say anything, but she's tugging on my ear so hard it almost comes off, and that wakes me. I can't see anything but the dark and the sparks of light from banging my head.

I try to sit up, but that turns out to be a bad idea because it makes me dizzy and I have to lie down again or puke. When I try to say something, Worm puts her hand on my mouth and shuts me up.

Footsteps. I can hear footsteps, and whispery voices.

"Must have gone this way," somebody whispers.

It's so completely dark I can't see a thing, but the voices have shapes. One belongs to the sheriff, the other to the Undertaker. And whenever *he* talks, Worm gets very, very quiet and still.

"No telling what evil things that boy has done," the Undertaker is saying in a voice so smooth it makes my brain itch. "He may have turned her mind against me."

The sheriff says, "Never mind that now. Get 'em out of this death trap alive, then we'll worry about sorting it all out."

The Undertaker doesn't like that. "The girl belongs to me," he insists. "Don't matter what happens to the boy."

It's hard to tell in the dark, but they sound real close, and getting closer. I'm thinking about what to do next when suddenly the whole tunnel *creeeaaaaaaks!* and the Undertaker shrieks out, "What's that?"

"Old timbers," the sheriff says. "They had a really bad cave-in here already, the same one that killed your stepdaughter's father. The rest of the place is ready to collapse any day now. Bump into the wrong timber and the mountain comes down on our heads."

"What do we do?" the Undertaker asks in a shaky voice.

"We get out of here before we make matters worse. Organize a search party. You were right about the girl heading here, but you gotta let me handle the police work, okay?"

The footsteps start to fade away. Then I hear the sheriff calling out, "Maxwell Kane, if you can hear me, listen up! Give yourself up and nobody gets hurt, not you or the girl. You've got my word on that!"

Me and the Worm keep still until the footsteps are gone. Until there's just us and the darkness and the wind in the tunnel.

When I try to stand up, my head gets bumped again, but not so hard this time. With my hands I can feel the busted timber sagging down from the roof of the tunnel. That's what clobbered me.

A light comes on, pointing right in my eyes.

Worm has turned on her miner's hat, and she's aiming it so I can see. Which should be good, right? Except the trouble is, now that I can see the rotten old timbers that hold up the tunnel, it makes me feel sick inside.

Here I am trying to keep Worm safe and we end up in a place that could bury us alive if we sneeze too hard.

"I'm not going back," Worm says, real fierce. "I don't care what happens, I'm never, ever going back to him."

I go, "We could get killed down here."

"You go on back," Worm says.

"The both of us," I say. "We'll go back together."

The light weaves as Worm shakes her head. "No way. I'd rather die."

Something in her voice makes me think she doesn't care if she does die, or maybe she even wants to, just to get away from being afraid. And that makes me decide to stick with her no matter what, even if my brain thinks I'm being stupid.

"We can't just stay here," I say. "They're coming back with a search party. They'll find us for sure."

"I told you. Go if you want to," Worm says, acting stubborn and fierce.

"That's not what I mean," I say. "Come on."

And then I take her hand and lead us deeper into the tunnel, into the dark places under the earth.

26.
Catch a Dragon by the Toe

The wind. That's what gives me the idea there might be another way out. The cool air sighing into my face. I figure it has to come from outside, and if we follow the wind we'll find it.

Worms sniffs at the air. "Smells like dragon breath," she says.

I go, "Huh?"

"Sulfur and rotten eggs."

I go, "Nah," but she's got me thinking about dragons and things that live in the dark, or die there.

It turns out there's more than one tunnel that goes down into the mine. There's like a maze deal going on, with tunnels branching off all over the place.

It reminds me of this ant farm I had once, until the ants got out and started snacking on Gram's homemade raspberry jam. Anyhow, before they escaped, the ants were digging a bunch of little tunnels and paths, and they kept streaming in and out, carrying grains of sand that were as big as boulders, if you happened to be an ant.

So I guess miners are like the human version of ants. They just keep digging until they find something good, and then they dig some more. They probably knew exactly where they were going, but I sure don't. It's not like they left behind signs that say THIS WAY TO ESCAPE or anything.

All we can do is follow the wind. And that's not easy because sometimes it's so faint you can barely feel the air moving, or you think it's your imagination and not the wind at all.

The Worm, she's got a talent for it. We'll be creeping along real slow and careful, making sure not to bump into timbers that hold up the roof, and then we'll come to a place where the tunnel branches off in two or three more directions. And Worm will stand there, her miner's hat shining like a lighthouse in the dark. She'll close her eyes and feel the air on her face, and then finally she'll point at the right tunnel.

At least I hope it's the right tunnel. Because the light-beam batteries aren't going to last forever, and even if Worm isn't scared of the dark, I am.

I figure once her light goes out, the whole mountain will probably come down on top of us. I can feel it all around me, how much the mine wants to bury us. Partly that's because I can't stand up straight, I have to move along hunched over. Whoever dug these tunnels made them for normal-sized people, not for me.

We're shuffling along, being careful not to bump into any of the old beams that hold up the mountain, when we come to another fork in the tunnel.

Worm shines her light into the tunnels but we can't see to the end. And I can't feel any air moving at all.

"Wait," Worm says, and she closes her eyes and tries to feel the wind on her face. When that doesn't work she starts counting off the way little kids do, except she does her own version. She goes, "Eenie-meenie-miney-moe, catch a dragon by the toe. If he saves us, let him go. Eenie-meenie-miney-moe."

"Are you serious?" I ask.

"It's better than just guessing," she says. "You got a better idea?"

I don't have a better idea, so we go down the "moe" tunnel. Which at first seems like all the other tunnels, with these rotten old timbers and boards holding up the roof, and piles of dirt and rock that have seeped down through the planks. But before we get very far, the floor starts getting damp. There are wet-looking streaks along the sides, and if you listen carefully you can hear the *bloink-bloink* of dripping water.

I go, "I dunno about this," because the dark is bad enough when it's dry, but Worm keeps scooting along and it's hard for me to keep up because the top of the tunnel keeps trying to wham me on the head. I'm going, "Hey, wait up!" but she won't slow down.

"We're almost there," she calls back. "I can feel it."

I go, "Slow down, please? I'm tired."

Worm finally slows down and waits for me to catch up. Which turns out to be a good thing. Because right around the next curve in the tunnel there's this big hole in the floor. At first I think it's just a shadow, but the Worm's light doesn't touch it and I go, "Whoa!" and pull her back from the edge just before we both fall in.

It's an old mine shaft going straight down into the deepest, darkest place in the world.

Worm aims her miner's hat into the hole, but the beam of light fades out before it hits bottom, that's how deep it is. When I drop a rock and listen for the clunk, there is no clunk. Like maybe the rock will keep falling forever, until it gets to the very center of the earth. There's an old ladder built into the side of the shaft, but some of the rungs are busted and you can see where the dampness has rotted up the wood.

"I bet that's where it happened," Worm says. "The cave-in. Way down there."

I don't know what to say. Maybe she's right,

maybe this is as close as she'll ever get to where her father died. I'm trying to think what it means to me when I visit my mom's grave in the cemetery. I always bring flowers, but today we don't have any flowers with us. We don't have much of anything.

"We could pray," I say, and Worm seems to like the idea. So we get down on our knees and fold up our hands, and when Worm nods her head to pray, her beam of light shines down into the shaft, and it looks scary and beautiful all at the same time.

Worm is praying silent, so I don't know exactly what she's thinking or saying inside her head. But whatever it is it seems to change her. She kind of relaxes all at once, like she's been waiting all her life to do this, and now that she's finally here she can let go and not be scared anymore.

I don't know what to pray, so I just thank God that her dad gave Worm the miner's light to find her way, because we sure would be lost without it.

When we're done, Worm gives my hand a squeeze and says, "Thanks."

Like a dummy I go, "Thanks for what?"

"For being Max the Mighty."

I go, "Look, I told you, there's no such thing as Max the Mighty. I'm just plain Maxwell Kane, okay?"

"Sure, okay. But when things got really bad I told myself Max the Mighty would come, and you did."

"I couldn't think of anything else to do," I say.

"I know," she says. "That's why you're Max the Mighty."

I'm about to tell her she's cracked in the brain if she really thinks that, but she goes, "Ssssh. We'll argue about it later. Right now we have to follow the wind. I can feel it, can you?"

I really *can* feel the wind. It smells cool and dry and it makes me think we're getting closer to the outside. Because I can't really explain it, but the air smells like it comes from the sky.

We edge around the mine shaft — there's barely enough room for my big fat feet — and head on up the tunnel.

"We'll come back here someday," she says. "You promise?"

I go, "Sure thing," but really I'm thinking *no way*. We get out of this place, I'm never coming back, not for all the TVs in China.

The tunnel starts to slope up and the wind feels even cooler and fresher, and I'm thinking, Way to go, you big goon, you were right for once in your life, maybe you aren't so dumb after all.

Then the tunnel starts getting wider, wide enough so the sides kind of melt away into the shadows, and I swear it's starting to get lighter. The roof part gets higher, too, and stops trying to wham me on the head, and it's all I can do to keep from running.

Easy does it, I'm thinking. *You're almost there.*

"Uh-oh," Worm says.

Uh-oh is right. Because suddenly the wind starts pushing hard against us, like something big is coming into the tunnel.

Worm goes, "The dragon! He's coming back!"

The ground starts shaking under my feet and the wind is coming faster and I can hear this low kind of growl, like a giant monster really has entered the tunnel, and we're in the way of where it wants to go.

Grrrruhhhhruhhhhhruhhhhhhh!

Coming to get us, making the shadows go crazy and filling the whole tunnel with wind and noise.

Then it starts to ROAR.

My brain keeps telling me, *There's no such thing as dragons*, but this sure sounds like one.

I pick Worm up and hold her tight so the wind doesn't blow her away. I'm so scared, my feet won't run.

That's when the glowing eyes find us. Eyes so bright they paint us with light. Eyes so bright it's like looking into the sun. Which must be what dragon eyes look like when they want to eat you up, or burn you to a crisp.

That's when I know we're going to die and there's nothing I can do about it.

27.
The Flower-Power Fogeys

Just before it kills us, the dragon honks.

I'm standing there like a total doughnut head, holding tight to Worm because we're dragon bait, we're history, when the monster with shining eyes honks at us.

Then it beeps.

I'm pretty sure dragons don't honk and I'm completely positive they don't beep. Cars beep, trucks beep.

Buses beep.

My brain has barely figured it out when Dip leaps out of the Prairie Schooner and gives us both a hug.

"Howdy doody, kids! Man, are we glad to see you!"

By now my eyes have gotten used to the headlights and I can see the old painted-up school bus filling up the tunnel. And behind Dip is this other old dude I can't quite make out. He's coming at us real careful, like he's afraid we'll disappear, or run away.

"Max," he says, and then I know.

It's Grim, my grandfather, which is like impossible. I'm so confused about how he could be here with the Dippy Hippie, or why the Prairie Schooner came roaring into the mine like a mean old dragon, that I can't think of anything to say.

Grim, he's not too cool with words either, so he just gives me this stiff kind of hug, and then he clears his throat and says, "Well. So. Fancy meeting you here, huh?"

It feels like I swallowed an apple or something, my throat is that choked up. Which is totally stupid because I should be happy, right? But instead it's like somebody punched me in the chest and I can hardly get my breath.

Dip, he takes charge and herds everybody into the bus. "We may have to make a sudden getaway," he says. Making it sound like a joke except it turns out he's not joking.

What happened is, after Frank and Joanie tried to turn us in for the reward and we had to run away or get arrested, Dip decided it was all his fault and he had to do something about it.

"Finally I did the right thing," Dip explains. "I called the police in your hometown and they gave me your grandfather's phone number. He hopped a plane and met me at a campground in Nebraska and we've been driving ever since." He looks over at stern-faced Grim and shakes his head. "Your grandpa is a funny old codger, but we get along okay."

Grim goes, "I'm no older than you are, you flower-power fogey." And Dip starts laughing so hard his glasses fall off and his big belly shakes. "That's it!" he says, "We're the flower-power fogeys!"

Grim makes a face and snorts, but you can tell he kind of likes the idea even if he won't admit it.

"We heard you'd been sighted in Chivalry, and when we got here the sheriff told us you'd run down into the old mining tunnels," Dip explains. "We thought you were goners, both of you. But we started searching for another way into the mine and got lucky. Then what do you know, our prayers were answered and you're both okay."

Worm has flopped down on the old sofa, testing the springs, and when Dip mentions the part about prayers being answered, she grins like crazy and her eyes are so bright and green you can hardly stand to look at her.

Grim clears his throat and goes, "Anybody got any ideas?"

"I hadn't really thought beyond finding these two," Dip whispers to him.

Grim nods to himself. "At this point it's their

word against, uhm, that man," he says very quietly.

Dip fiddles with one of his pigtails like he does when he's thinking hard. After a while he goes, "We need to find Max a good lawyer. I've got a little money saved up and you're welcome to it."

"We'll manage," Grim says. "But thanks."

The amazing thing is, somehow they both know I didn't do anything wrong, even without me telling them. Which makes me think if you stick to the truth you'll be okay, even if the rest of the world thinks you're a liar.

Dip brightens up and says, "I've got another idea." We're all expecting something really amazing, but he says, "One word. Pancakes."

Grim grumbles and goes, "That's your big idea?"

"These kids look half-starved," Dip points out. "We'll all think better on full stomachs. So I vote we head for the nearest pancake house, eat till we bust, and then we'll figure out what to do next."

"Pancakes sound good," Worm says.

Dip says it's settled and he fires up the Prairie Schooner and backs it out of the tunnel, going extra careful so he doesn't scratch the paint, which probably nobody but him would notice.

When we're almost out of the tunnel the back windows start to turn orange, which looks weird until I realize the sun is going down. So me and Worm were lost in the mine for a whole day. If you asked me how long it was, I'd have said some-where between ten minutes and forever.

I'm thinking the sunset is pretty cool, the way the sky looks on fire, and the clouds could be giant castles made of smoke, when all of a sudden Dip says a bad word and jams on the brakes.

Grim goes, "Everybody stay calm," but there's no way I can stay calm when I see the white cop car blocking our way.

Dip is tapping his fingers on the wheel and looking in the rearview mirror and saying, "Darn. I really had my heart set on pancakes."

My stomach feels like I've been eating tadpoles again, which I haven't done since I was too dumb to know any better, but my stomach doesn't know that, and my brain is having a great time laughing at me. *You big moron*, it says. *What did you expect? A happy ending? Did you really think you could drive off into the sunset and nothing would happen? Huh? Are you really that stupid? Answer me, you big moron.*

I want to tell my brain to shut up, but it's too late, Sheriff Goodman is already knocking on the door of the bus.

"Open up!" he says. "I want you all to come out real peaceful. One at a time. No sudden moves and no fooling around."

Dip opens the bus door. "No problem," he says to the sheriff.

Dip gets out first. Then Grim. Then me. The

sheriff is giving me this look, like if he stares hard enough the truth will just melt right out of me.

Grim goes, "There's been a mistake, officer. Max never meant any harm. He was trying to protect the girl. Her stepfather is the real culprit."

"Could be," the sheriff says. "That's for a court to decide."

He unsnaps a pair of handcuffs from his belt. "Maxwell Kane, you're under arrest."

The weird thing is, even though I should feel really terrible and low and miserable, I don't. Not even close. I'm too happy that Grim and Dip are there to take care of Worm, and anyhow, sleeping in a jail cell can't be much worse than sleeping in a freight car or an old saloon with holes in the roof, and I did both of those and came out okay. I'm thinking maybe prison won't be so bad after all, and they'll probably let me read books and maybe I'll take up a hobby and be the Bird Man of Alka-Seltzer or whatever.

"Hold out your hands," the sheriff tells me.

He's just about to put the cuffs on me when the cop car door creaks open. "I told you to stay in the car," the sheriff says, real sharp.

But the Undertaker gets out anyhow. With his black clothes and his black hat. His face is pointed like a hatchet and his eyes are full of hate.

He comes barging up, jamming his finger at me like a gun. "Where is she?" he shouts, spit flying from his mouth. "What have you done with

Rachel? You've been brainwashing her, haven't you? Turning her against me!"

That's when Worm sneaks out of the bus, holding her bag of books. She tries to hide behind me, but the Undertaker makes a grab at her and she ducks away. She won't look at him, no matter what.

"Rachel?" he says.

"I'm not Rachel!" she shouts. "Rachel is dead!"

Then Worm moves so quick that nobody can stop her.

I go, "No! Don't!"

But it's too late. The darkness has already swallowed her up.

28.
Suddenly Worm Says Good-bye

Only a total moron would run into a deep dark mine without a flashlight. But I don't have time to think about it, because I know where Worm is going.

The mine shaft. The place where we prayed and she felt she was safe from all the bad things in the world, and nothing could touch her.

I've got this terrible empty feeling inside, like that falling dream you have just before you go to sleep, only I'm wide-awake and it won't stop.

"Rachel!" I'm calling out. "Wait up! Wait for me!"

But her running feet keep skittering ahead of me in the darkness. The thing is, because I have to scrunch down to keep from bumping my head, Worm can run a lot faster than me. And even scrunched over, I keep banging into things, the sides of the tunnel and the timbers and stuff.

I'm not the only one chasing Worm. The others are back there behind me. Grim and Dip and Sheriff Goodman and the Undertaker, too. Which makes me run all the faster, because if *he* gets to her first, there's no telling what will happen.

Running faster turns out to be a mistake. *Smack!* Before I know what's happening, I'm flat on my back with my nose swelling up like a banana where I smacked it against the wall. Fork in the tunnel and I hit it face first.

So now I've got two tunnels to choose from and no time to mess around. I try to shake the ringing out of my ears and listen for those running feet. *Pitter-pat, pitter-pat.* Hide-and-seek, except for her it's just the hide part. She doesn't want anybody to find her, not ever.

Go right, my brain tells me.

The tunnel slopes down pretty steep, which makes sense because when we came from the opposite direction it slanted up. Up toward the light. Down into the darkness.

"Rachel! Please wait!"

That's when I notice a faint beam of light flickering far ahead. Worm has her miner's light on. Which makes me feel a little better because at least she won't fall into the mine shaft, not if she can see it first.

Or that's what I'm hoping. That's what keeps me going, even though I can't seem to get enough air to breathe and my feet feel like they're made of lead. Mostly what's wrong with me is I'm afraid. Afraid Worm is going to get hurt or killed and it'll be my fault.

Your fault? my brain says. *Don't be a bonehead. How could it be your fault?*

Because I made her think I'd keep her safe, and then I didn't, that's why. Because even though I said there was no such thing as Max the Mighty, I really thought there was, and it turned out to be a lie.

But you didn't mean to hurt her, my brain says.

So what? It's still my fault, I'm thinking. If you want to be a superhero, you have to get it right, that's the deal.

I'm thinking so hard my feet get tangled up and I go down, skidding along the slanted floor, getting closer and closer to the flickering light.

When I finally come to a stop, I put my hands out to push myself up from the floor, but there is no floor.

I'm right on the edge of the mine shaft.

Inch by inch I wriggle backward until I'm clear of the edge and my heart can start beating again.

"You shouldn't have come," Worm says. "I have to do this by myself."

At first I can't see her. All I can see is the miner's light bobbing around. After a while I can make out a shadow that has the shape of her, and that's when my heart wants to stop again, because she's standing right on the edge of the mine shaft.

"Be careful," I say. "You'll fall in."

"So what?" She says softly. "My dad is dead. My mom might as well be dead, married to a creep like that. Things would be a whole lot easier if I was dead, too."

She's on the other side of the shaft, where I can't get to her right away.

Say something, my brain tells me.

I want to tell her that life is like the books she reads, and no matter how bad things look, it will all work out in the end. That's another big lie, but I'll say anything to stop her from going over the edge. The problem is, I'm so scared that my mouth won't work.

"I know you tried," she says. "And I kept pretending it would be okay. But it isn't okay. He'll get me. Nobody can stop him."

I'm on my hands and knees, creeping along in slow motion, no sudden moves. But the closer I get to her, the closer she gets to the edge.

I go, "Max the Mighty can stop him. Max the Mighty can save you."

She moves even closer to the edge. "There's no such thing," she says. "I made it up, remember?"

That stops me in my tracks. Because I know in my bones that if I don't have an answer, Worm will slip over the edge. And it has to be the right answer and it has to be true.

I'm kind of surprised when my mouth starts talking, like it already knows what to say without me having to think about it.

"You're right," I say. "You made it up. I'm just plain Max, and I'll never read as many books as you, or be as smart as you, but I do know one thing. You know how bad you feel about your father, and how much you miss him? I feel that bad about my mom and my best friend Kevin. And if I lose you, I'll feel even worse, all the time. Every day for the rest of my life. And that's the truth."

I'm staring across the mine shaft at her miner's light. Staring with all my might, hoping I said the right thing.

Suddenly Worm says, "Good-bye," and then the miner's light is falling. It spins end over end, falling down and down and down, getting smaller and smaller, until the darkness swallows it up, and I'm all alone in the dark.

Inside it feels like part of me is falling with the light, and will keep falling forever.

Stupid, stupid, STUPID.

And then a warm hand finds my big stupid face in the dark and Worm says, "I gave my father back his light. So he can find his way in the dark, like I did."

I've got Worm by the hand and we're going slow and careful, heading up through the shadows to the surface of the world.

She's afraid but that doesn't stop her. "You've got to promise," she says. "Friends for life. No matter what. No matter how many fights we have or how many stupid things we say to each other."

"I hate fights," I say. "But I can't help saying stupid things sometimes."

"But you promise?"

I go, "Promise," and then Worm asks me to crouch down and she gives me a quick little kiss.

"For luck," she explains. "We're going to need it."

We're coming into the rosy light of sunset when the ground starts shaking under our feet.

Rrrrrrrrrummmmble.

Like the whole mine is clearing its throat and getting ready to cough. There's a sound like wood splitting, and then something heavy falls *thump!* and makes the ground shake again.

Up ahead of us, not too far away, somebody groans.

"Help . . . me," a familiar voice says. "Help me or I'll die."

29.
The End of Maxwell Kane

All I can see of the Undertaker is his long, black-covered legs sticking out from under a huge beam. Part of the mine has caved in and he's trapped. His boots are twitching so I know he's alive.

"I can't breathe," he gasps. "Get this off me, please."

Feet come running up behind us.

"Don't touch anything," Sheriff Goodman says. "The whole place is ready to come down on our heads."

Dip and Grim are both panting so hard they can barely talk, but Grim sees Worm is safe and sound and he gives me a thumbs-up. Which is pretty cool for Grim.

The Undertaker groans some more. The way the beam has got him pinned, I can't see his face, but I can hear him moaning and groaning, and it sure sounds pitiful. Even though I can't stand the guy, I feel bad for him, the way you'd feel if a really mean dog got hit by a car and needed help. Part of you is glad the dog can't hurt you anymore, but you don't want it to die.

I go, "Maybe we can dig out from under him," but the sheriff thinks that's a bad idea, that it might make matters worse.

"Everybody out of the mine," he says. "I'll call backup, get a rescue team in here to do it right."

"Don't leave me!" the Undertaker wails.

Worm, she's been standing there real quiet, not moving. But after a little while she lets go of my hand and edges a little closer to him. Not too close, like she's worried he's playing a trick.

"You were the one who beat up my mom," she says. "You were the one who hurt me. It was you! Not Max. You lied about that. You lied about everything."

The Undertaker groans and then goes, "Your momma was asking for it! She was going to call the cops! It was all her fault!"

When Sheriff Goodman hears that, he looks at me and nods, like he knew all along that I wasn't really a criminal. Then he tugs down on the brim of his cowboy hat and says, "Let's move along, folks."

We're starting to go when suddenly I can feel it coming up through my feet. This rumbling from deep underground, like the whole mine has decided to cave in, starting at the bottom.

"Please!" the Undertaker groans. "Somebody help!"

The timbers and planks are shaking. Clouds of dust belch up from down below.

Creeeeak! And a huge *kerchunk!* of rocks smashing together. Everything is breaking, falling apart.

"She's going!" the sheriff cries. "Get out of here! Run!"

Dip grabs hold of Worm and takes her away and I can hear Grim shouting at me through the roaring dust. Shouting to leave while I've got the chance.

There's nothing I want more than to get out of that mine while the getting is good, but just as I start to go, a strange thing happens.

This pale white hand reaches up through the dirt and the dust. The Undertaker. He can't talk because his face is covered with dirt, but his hand is begging me for help. *Don't leave me*, it says. *Please, please.*

Grim screams, "Max! Don't!"

My brain screams, *Run! Run!*

But it's too late, because I've already got my arms under the fallen beam, and I'm yanking it up with all my might. With so many rocks pinning it down, it must weigh a ton. It's like trying to move the earth, but I have to do it, there's no one else who can.

So I yank harder. Harder.

The beam moves.

The thing is, once you start lifting something really heavy, you can't stop when you're half-way done. You have to lift it all the way up. My knees feel like old tires about to blow out, but I can't stop until the huge old timber is up on my shoulder.

Grim screams, "Got him!" and drags the Undertaker out and helps him to his feet.

Then the ground is shaking again. Dust blows down from the ceiling and timbers start popping out of the walls, snapping like toothpicks.

Of course I want to let go of that beam and run, but it's like I'm pinned to the ground by the weight of everything. Stuff is coming loose all around me but I can't move. All I can do is keep holding up the timber and the roof above it and the mountain above that. Which nobody can do, not even a big huge doofus like me.

The last thing I remember is how much it sounds like the ocean. Like waves crashing, and seagulls screaming, and gravel caught in the undertow. The dust is real bad, but I can make out a couple of shadowy figures running toward the light, and I'm glad Worm is okay, and Grim and Dip got out in time. This is really dumb, but it doesn't even bother me about the Undertaker getting out alive.

I'm thinking this is the end for Maxwell Kane,

too bad he never got a chance to be Max the Mighty, and that's when the beam finally slips and the whole world crashes down on me and it really is the end, the end,

the end.

30.
After the End

They say Grim and Dip and Sheriff Goodman dug through all that dirt until their hands were bleeding, and finally got me out in one piece, more or less, and that I kept saying something really stupid like, "I hear the ocean, I hear the ocean." I don't remember because I was so out of it.

When I woke up in the hospital, this nurse told me I'd broken my shoulder and my leg, and could she please autograph my cast, which I thought was pretty weird, her being a nurse and all.

Then Grim and Gram came in, and Grim said he guessed I wouldn't be dancing in the ballet, on account of my leg. That's his idea of a joke, ha ha.

Worm, she was real upset with her mom for going along with all the Undertaker's lies, even though she was so scared of him she couldn't help it. But then she felt a lot better about everything when her mom finally got up the courage and testified in court about what really happened, and the Undertaker got convicted.

It turns out he'd done the same kind of creepy stuff to another kid and her mother years before, and so he's going to be in prison a long, long time, which is just fine by me.

The best thing is that Gram made a big fuss and insisted that Worm and her mom come live with us, at least for a while, until they get on their own two feet again. Gram said she and Grim had always wanted to have a big family, and this was the chance of a lifetime.

At first Worm's mom said she couldn't possibly, but Gram wouldn't take no for an answer, and now Worm's mom says that moving in with us was the best thing for all concerned, and even though Grim is an opinionated old coot, she wouldn't trade him for the world.

So the way it all worked out, now I've got a little sister for the time being, and who knows, maybe forever. Which is pretty cool, if I do say so myself.

Sometimes when I get bored and there's nothing to do in the down under and we're out of books to read, I ask Worm if she wants to do it all over again. Just stick out our thumbs and see where the road takes us.

You know, have another cool adventure.

When I say that, Worm looks at me and goes,

"Are you cracked?" Then she'll kid me and say why don't I grow up and get a brain like normal people?

That's when I tell her I'll never be normal, not in a million years, and I like it that way just fine, thank you.

And that's the truth. The unvanquished truth.

About This Point Signature Author

RODMAN PHILBRICK is the award-winning author of two previous novels for young readers. His first novel, *Freak the Mighty* (Blue Sky Press, 1993), was received with great acclaim, appearing on numerous state award lists, and has been made into THE MIGHTY, a Miramax feature film. His second novel for young adults, *The Fire Pony* (Blue Sky Press, 1996), received the 1996 Capital Choice Award and a pointed review in *Kirkus Reviews*.

Philbrick and his wife, also a writer, divide their time between Maine and the Florida Keys.